The Forgotten City

Fairy tales, Folk tales, Legends & Mythology, Volume 7

Patrick William Lee

Published by Starlit Tales Publishing, 2024.

This is a work of fiction. Similarities to real people, places, or events are entirely coincidental.

THE FORGOTTEN CITY

First edition. September 3, 2024.

Copyright © 2024 Patrick William Lee.

ISBN: 979-8227688019

Written by Patrick William Lee.

Table of Contents

To the seekers of wisdom and the dreamers of ancient worlds,

This story is for those who believe that true power lies not in wealth or might, but in the knowledge we pass on and the lessons we learn from the past. May the legacy of forgotten cities remind us all that our greatest treasures are the stories we live and share.

With gratitude to the countless storytellers, past and present, who keep the flames of imagination and history burning bright.

— Patrick William Lee

Chapter 1: The Prophecy of the Hidden Realm

The Night of Whispers

The wind howled through the narrow streets of Duncaster, a small, forgotten village nestled deep in the shadow of the great Blackstone Mountains. The village had always been shrouded in an air of mystery, its history steeped in tales of ancient magic and forgotten realms. On nights like this, when the moon hid behind a thick curtain of clouds and the wind carried with it the chilling touch of the mountains, the villagers would gather in the warmth of their hearths, eager to share tales passed down through generations.

This night, however, was different. There was an unease in the air, a feeling that something ancient had awakened. The villagers could sense it, though they dared not speak of it. Instead, they huddled closer around their fires, their voices hushed as they recounted the old stories, none more captivating than the tale of the forgotten city and the prophecy that foretold its rediscovery.

In the largest of the village's cottages, the elders gathered. They were the keepers of the village's history, the custodians of its lore. Their faces were lined with age, their eyes filled with the knowledge of years long past. Tonight, they had come together to discuss the prophecy, for they had all felt the same disturbance in the air, the same tug at the edge of their consciousness.

Elder Mirela, the oldest and most respected among them, was the first to speak. Her voice, though frail with age, still carried the weight of authority. "The winds have shifted," she said, her tone grave. "The mountains stir, and with them, the prophecy awakens."

The other elders nodded in agreement, their faces etched with concern. They had all felt it—an ancient presence, something old and powerful that had been dormant for centuries but was now stirring once more.

1

"It has been many generations since the prophecy was first spoken," said Elder Thane, his deep voice resonating through the room. "But its words have not been forgotten. They have been passed down, from one elder to the next, waiting for the time when they would come to pass."

Elder Mirela nodded, her eyes distant as she recalled the prophecy. "A city hidden in the mountains," she murmured. "A place where time stands still, where the secrets of a lost civilization lie buried. And only the chosen one, marked by the symbol of destiny, can unlock its mysteries."

The room fell silent as the elders pondered the implications of the prophecy. They had all heard it before, countless times, but now it felt different. Now it felt real.

"But who is this chosen one?" asked Elder Brynn, her voice tinged with fear. "How will we know when they have arrived?"

Elder Mirela sighed, her old eyes weary. "The prophecy speaks of a mark, a symbol that will appear on the chosen one's skin. It is said to be a sign from the gods, a mark that cannot be ignored."

The elders exchanged uneasy glances. A mark from the gods? It was a terrifying thought, one that filled them with both dread and anticipation. For if the prophecy was true, then the arrival of the chosen one would herald a new era, one that could either bring great prosperity or unimaginable destruction.

"We must be vigilant," Elder Thane declared, his voice firm. "If the chosen one is among us, we must find them. The fate of our village, perhaps even the world, may depend on it."

The elders nodded in agreement, their resolve strengthened. They knew what they had to do. The prophecy had been awakened, and with it, their duty to protect their village and the secrets of the forgotten city.

The Village of Duncaster

DUNCASTER WAS NOT AN ordinary village. Its location, deep within the Blackstone Mountains, meant it was isolated from the rest of the world. Few travelers ventured into the mountains, and even fewer returned. The village itself was small, consisting of little more than a few dozen cottages, a communal hall, and a single well from which the villagers drew their water. The people of Duncaster were a hardy folk, accustomed to the harsh winters and the rugged terrain. They were farmers, herders, and craftsmen, their lives simple but fulfilling.

Yet, despite its small size and remote location, Duncaster was not without its share of mysteries. The villagers spoke of strange occurrences, of whispers carried on the wind, of shadows that moved on their own. They spoke of ancient ruins hidden in the mountains, remnants of a civilization long forgotten. And they spoke of the prophecy, always in hushed tones, as if afraid to give it life by speaking of it too loudly.

For centuries, the prophecy had been little more than a story, a tale told to frighten children or to pass the time on long winter nights. But now, with the winds changing and the mountains stirring, the prophecy had taken on a new significance. The villagers could feel it in their bones, a sense of impending change that they could not ignore.

Elara was one such villager. She was young, barely seventeen, with long dark hair that cascaded down her back like a waterfall of midnight. Her eyes were a deep, piercing blue, and her skin was fair, almost translucent in the moonlight. Elara was not like the other villagers. She was different, though she could never quite put her finger on why. She had always felt a connection to the mountains, a pull that she could not explain. It was as if the mountains were calling to her, beckoning her to uncover their secrets.

Elara lived with her mother, a kind but stern woman named Liora. They lived in a small cottage on the edge of the village, near the base of the mountains. Liora was a healer, known throughout the village for her knowledge of herbs and potions. She had raised Elara on her own, her husband having died when Elara was just a baby. Liora had never spoken much about Elara's father, and Elara had long since stopped asking. She knew that it was a painful subject for her mother, and so she had learned to keep her curiosity to herself.

But there was one thing that Elara could never ignore: the mark on her wrist. It had been there for as long as she could remember, a small, intricate symbol that seemed to glow faintly in the moonlight. Liora had always told her to keep it hidden, to never show it to anyone, and Elara had obeyed, though she had often wondered why. The mark had never caused her any pain or discomfort, but it had always felt significant, as if it were a part of her destiny.

Tonight, as the wind howled outside and the village elders gathered to discuss the prophecy, Elara lay in her bed, staring at the mark on her wrist.

She traced the lines of the symbol with her finger, feeling a strange warmth emanating from it. The warmth spread through her body, filling her with a sense of calm and purpose. She knew that something was about to change, that her life was about to take a new direction. But what that direction was, she could not yet say.

The Legend of the Forgotten City

THE LEGEND OF THE FORGOTTEN city was an old one, older than the village of Duncaster itself. It was said that the city had once been the heart of a great civilization, a place of knowledge and power where the gods themselves had walked among men. The city had been a place of beauty and wonder, its streets lined with golden statues and its buildings adorned with intricate carvings. The people of the city had been wise and learned, their minds filled with the secrets of the universe.

But as with all great civilizations, the city had fallen. The reasons for its downfall were lost to time, but the legend spoke of a great cataclysm, a disaster that had wiped the city from the face of the earth. The people had perished, their knowledge and power lost forever. The city itself had been swallowed by the mountains, hidden away from the world, its secrets buried deep within the earth.

Yet the legend did not end there. It was said that the city still existed, hidden away in a realm where time stood still. The city had not been destroyed, but merely forgotten, waiting for the day when it would be rediscovered. And with its rediscovery, the secrets of the lost civilization would be revealed once more.

But there was more to the legend than just the city itself. There was the prophecy, a tale that had been passed down through the generations, spoken of in hushed tones by the village elders. The prophecy spoke of a chosen one, a person marked by the gods who would one day unlock the mysteries of the forgotten city. This chosen one would bear a symbol, a mark that would appear on their skin, a sign that they were destined to fulfill the prophecy.

The villagers had always taken the legend and the prophecy with a grain of salt. They were stories, nothing more. But now, with the winds shifting and the mountains stirring, the prophecy had taken on a new significance. The villagers could feel it in their bones, a sense of impending change that they could not ignore.

The Awakening of the Prophecy

AS THE ELDERS DISCUSSED the prophecy in their meeting, the winds outside began to pick up, howling through the narrow streets of Duncaster. The temperature dropped, and a thick fog rolled in from the mountains, enveloping the village in a blanket of mist. The villagers shivered, pulling their cloaks tighter around themselves as they hurried home, eager to escape the cold.

In her cottage, Elara felt the change in the air. She could feel the wind tugging at her soul, calling her to the mountains. She sat up in bed, her heart pounding in her chest as the warmth in her wrist intensified. The mark on her wrist began to glow, the symbol becoming more defined, more pronounced. Elara gasped, clutching her wrist as the warmth spread through her body, filling her with a sense of urgency.

She had to go to the mountains. She didn't know why, but she knew she had to go. The mountains were calling her, beckoning her to uncover their secrets. She swung her legs out of bed, her bare feet touching the cold stone floor. She dressed quickly, pulling on her warmest clothes and wrapping a thick cloak around her shoulders. She slipped on her boots and grabbed her satchel, filling it with a few essentials—bread, cheese, a flask of water, and a small knife.

As she prepared to leave, a thought crossed her mind. She couldn't just leave without telling her mother. But how could she explain the urgency she felt, the pull towards the mountains that she couldn't ignore? She hesitated, her hand on the door handle, torn between her duty to her mother and the overwhelming need to follow the call of the mountains.

But before she could make a decision, the door creaked open, and Liora stepped into the room. Elara froze, her heart pounding in her chest as she met her mother's gaze. Liora's face was pale, her eyes wide with a mixture of fear and understanding.

"You feel it too, don't you?" Liora's voice was barely above a whisper, but it carried the weight of a thousand unspoken words.

Elara nodded, unable to find her voice. The warmth in her wrist intensified, the glow from the mark casting a soft light in the dim room.

Liora stepped closer, her eyes locked on the glowing mark on Elara's wrist. She reached out, gently tracing the lines of the symbol with her finger. "I always knew this day would come," she murmured, her voice filled with a mixture of sorrow and pride.

Elara looked at her mother in confusion. "You knew?"

Liora nodded, tears welling up in her eyes. "Your father... he knew too. Before you were born, he had a vision. He saw this mark, this symbol, and he knew what it meant. He knew you were destined for something greater, something beyond this village."

Elara's heart ached at the mention of her father. She had always felt his absence, a void in her life that could never be filled. "What happened to him?" she asked, her voice trembling.

Liora sighed, her shoulders sagging with the weight of the memories. "He went to the mountains, just like you're about to do. He believed in the prophecy, in the legend of the forgotten city. He wanted to protect you, to ensure that you would fulfill your destiny. But he never returned."

Elara felt a surge of emotion—anger, sadness, fear, and determination all at once. She wanted to ask more, to demand answers, but there was no time. The call of the mountains was too strong, too urgent to ignore.

"I have to go," Elara said, her voice firm despite the turmoil in her heart.

Liora nodded, her tears falling freely now. "I know. And I can't stop you. But promise me one thing—promise me you'll come back."

Elara stepped forward, wrapping her arms around her mother in a tight embrace. "I promise, Mother. I'll come back."

Liora held her daughter close, her heart breaking at the thought of losing her, just as she had lost her husband. But she knew she couldn't stop Elara, just as she hadn't been able to stop her husband. The prophecy was in motion, and there was no turning back.

The Journey Begins

THE NIGHT WAS COLD and dark as Elara stepped out of her cottage and into the foggy streets of Duncaster. The village was silent, the only sound the howling wind and the distant creaking of wooden signs swaying in the breeze.

Elara pulled her cloak tighter around her, her breath visible in the frigid air as she made her way towards the mountains.

The path was steep and treacherous, winding its way through dense forests and rocky terrain. Elara's heart pounded in her chest as she climbed higher and higher, the fog thickening around her until she could barely see a few feet in front of her. But she pressed on, driven by the warmth in her wrist and the unshakable sense of purpose that had taken hold of her.

As she ascended the mountain, the fog began to thin, revealing the craggy peaks of the Blackstone Mountains in the distance. The wind whipped through the trees, carrying with it a low, mournful howl that seemed to echo through the valleys. Elara shivered, both from the cold and the eerie atmosphere, but she refused to turn back.

The journey was long and arduous, but Elara was no stranger to hardship. She had grown up in the mountains, had spent her childhood exploring the forests and learning the ways of the land. She knew how to navigate the treacherous terrain, how to find shelter and food when needed. But this journey was different. There was an urgency to it, a sense of danger that kept her on edge, always alert to the slightest sound or movement.

As the night wore on, Elara found herself growing weary. Her legs ached from the climb, her breath coming in ragged gasps as she pushed herself to keep going. The warmth in her wrist had faded, replaced by a dull ache that spread through her entire body. But she refused to stop, knowing that she had to reach the forgotten city before it was too late.

Finally, after what felt like hours of relentless climbing, Elara reached a plateau overlooking a vast, mist-shrouded valley. She paused, leaning against a boulder to catch her breath, her eyes scanning the horizon for any sign of the forgotten city.

But there was nothing. The valley stretched out before her, empty and desolate, the mist swirling around the jagged peaks like a living thing. Elara's heart sank, doubt creeping into her mind. Had she come all this way for nothing? Was the prophecy just a story, a legend with no basis in reality?

But just as she was about to turn back, something caught her eye. A faint glimmer of light, barely visible through the mist, flickering like a distant star. Elara's heart leaped in her chest, hope surging through her as she realized that the light was coming from the valley below.

With renewed determination, Elara began her descent into the valley, the light guiding her like a beacon in the darkness. The path was steep and treacherous, the rocks slick with moisture, but Elara moved with the surefootedness of someone who had spent her life in the mountains. The light grew brighter as she descended, until it became a steady, glowing presence that lit her way through the mist.

Finally, after what felt like an eternity, Elara reached the bottom of the valley. The mist parted before her, revealing a sight that took her breath away.

Before her stood the forgotten city.

The Forgotten City Revealed

THE CITY WAS LIKE NOTHING Elara had ever seen. Its buildings were tall and majestic, their walls made of a smooth, gleaming stone that seemed to glow with an inner light. The architecture was unlike anything she had encountered in Duncaster or in the surrounding villages—elegant, intricate, and awe-inspiring. The streets were wide and paved with the same gleaming stone, winding their way through the city like rivers of light.

But the city was not untouched by time. Though it stood in stark contrast to the rugged wilderness around it, there were signs of decay. Vines and moss clung to the walls, creeping up the sides of buildings and spilling over the edges of balconies. The once-pristine streets were cracked and uneven in places, and some of the buildings had crumbled, their ruins lying in heaps of stone and dust.

Elara stepped forward, her heart pounding in her chest as she took in the sight before her. She had found it—the forgotten city that had existed only in legends and whispers. And yet, standing here now, it felt more real than anything she had ever known.

She wandered through the streets, her eyes wide with wonder as she took in the details of the city. The carvings on the buildings depicted scenes of a civilization at the height of its power—great battles, majestic creatures, and gods bestowing their blessings upon the people. Elara felt as if she had stepped into another world, a world that had been frozen in time, waiting for her to discover it.

As she explored the city, Elara couldn't shake the feeling that she was being watched. The hairs on the back of her neck stood on end, and she found herself glancing over her shoulder every few steps, half-expecting to see a shadowy figure lurking in the distance. But there was nothing—only the silent, empty streets and the towering buildings that loomed over her like silent sentinels.

Finally, she came to a large square in the center of the city. In the middle of the square stood a massive statue, carved from the same gleaming stone as the rest of the city. The statue depicted a figure draped in flowing robes, their hands raised in a gesture of blessing. The figure's face was serene, their eyes closed as if in prayer.

But it was not the statue itself that drew Elara's attention—it was the base of the statue, where a familiar symbol was etched into the stone. It was the same symbol that was on her wrist, the same intricate design that had glowed with warmth and guided her to this place.

Elara stepped closer, her breath catching in her throat as she reached out to touch the symbol. The moment her fingers made contact with the stone, a surge of energy shot through her, filling her with a sense of power and purpose. The symbol on her wrist began to glow once more, the light spreading from her hand to the statue, illuminating the entire square with a soft, golden light.

The ground beneath her feet began to tremble, and Elara stumbled back, her heart racing as the statue's eyes slowly opened. The figure's serene expression remained unchanged, but their eyes were now glowing with the same light that emanated from the symbol.

"Welcome, chosen one," a voice echoed through the square, deep and resonant, yet gentle and soothing.

Elara's eyes widened in shock as she realized that the voice was coming from the statue itself. "Who... who are you?" she stammered, her voice trembling.

"I am the guardian of this city," the statue replied, its voice carrying a weight of ancient wisdom. "I have awaited your arrival for many centuries, chosen one. You are the one foretold in the prophecy, the one who will unlock the secrets of the forgotten city and restore its glory."

Elara's mind raced as she tried to process the statue's words. "But... why me? Why was I chosen?"

The statue's eyes glowed brighter, and the ground beneath Elara's feet seemed to pulse with energy. "You bear the mark of destiny, the symbol of the gods. It is a sign that you are destined to fulfill the prophecy, to uncover the secrets of this lost civilization and bring its knowledge back to the world."

Elara's heart pounded in her chest, a mixture of fear and excitement flooding her senses. "But what does the prophecy mean? What secrets are hidden here?"

The statue's expression softened, and its voice took on a more solemn tone. "This city was once the heart of a great civilization, a place of unparalleled knowledge and power. But that power became its downfall. The people of this city sought to control the forces of nature, to bend the will of the gods to their own desires. In their arrogance, they unleashed a cataclysm that brought about their destruction. The city was swallowed by the mountains, hidden away from the world, its secrets buried deep within the earth."

Elara listened in rapt attention, her mind racing as she absorbed the statue's words.

"The gods, in their mercy, spared the city from complete annihilation," the statue continued. "They placed it in a realm where time stands still, preserving it until the day when a chosen one would come to unlock its secrets and learn from its mistakes. That day has come, and you are the chosen one, Elara."

Elara's breath caught in her throat at the sound of her name. "You... you know who I am?"

The statue's eyes seemed to soften, and a faint smile touched its lips. "I have watched over you since the day you were born. Your father was a great man, Elara, a man who understood the importance of the prophecy. He knew that you were destined for greatness, that you would be the one to fulfill the prophecy and restore the balance that was lost so long ago."

Tears welled up in Elara's eyes as she thought of her father, the man she had never known but who had shaped her destiny in ways she could never have imagined. "What do I have to do?" she asked, her voice barely above a whisper.

"The journey will not be easy," the statue replied. "You must unlock the secrets of this city, one by one, and learn from the mistakes of those who came before you. Only then can you restore the balance and bring the knowledge of this lost civilization back to the world."

Elara nodded, her resolve hardening. She had come this far, and she would not turn back now. She would fulfill the prophecy, uncover the secrets of the forgotten city, and restore its glory.

"Where do I begin?" she asked, her voice filled with determination.

The statue's eyes glowed brighter, and the ground beneath Elara's feet began to tremble once more. "Your journey begins in the Temple of Forgotten Gods," the statue said. "There, you will receive the blessings of the ancient deities who once protected this city. But be warned, Elara—each god will present you with a challenge, a test of your strength, wisdom, and compassion. Only by passing these tests can you unlock the secrets of the temple and continue on your journey."

Elara took a deep breath, steeling herself for the challenges that lay ahead. "I understand," she said. "I will do whatever it takes to fulfill the prophecy."

The statue's eyes softened, and the glowing light began to fade. "Good luck, chosen one," the statue said, its voice filled with a warmth that Elara had never felt before. "May the gods guide your path and grant you the strength to overcome the trials that await you."

With those words, the light faded completely, and the statue returned to its original, lifeless state. The square was once again shrouded in darkness, the only sound the faint rustling of the wind through the ruins of the city.

Elara stood alone in the square, her heart pounding with a mixture of fear and excitement. The journey ahead would be long and difficult, but she knew that she was ready. She had been chosen to fulfill the prophecy, to unlock the secrets of the forgotten city, and to bring its knowledge back to the world.

With a final glance at the statue, Elara turned and began her journey toward the Temple of Forgotten Gods, the first step on the path to uncovering the mysteries of the hidden realm.

Chapter 2: The Marked One

The Birthmark's Secret

The dawn broke over the village of Duncaster with a soft, golden light, illuminating the peaks of the Blackstone Mountains. The air was crisp and fresh, carrying the scent of pine and earth. The villagers were already awake, busy with their daily chores—tending to their livestock, mending fences, and preparing for the day ahead. But amidst the ordinary rhythm of life, an undercurrent of tension and excitement buzzed through the community.

Elara, a young villager barely seventeen years old, was at the center of this growing storm. She had always been different, though she couldn't quite explain how or why. She was curious, more so than others her age, always seeking to understand the mysteries of the world around her. It wasn't just her insatiable curiosity that set her apart—it was also the strange birthmark on her wrist, a small, intricate symbol that had been there since she was born.

For as long as she could remember, her mother, Liora, had warned her to keep the birthmark hidden. "It's not something to be shown to others," Liora would say, her voice tinged with a mix of concern and fear. Elara had never fully understood why, but she had obeyed. She had grown accustomed to wearing long sleeves or wrapping her wrist with a cloth, making sure no one in the village ever saw the mark.

But now, with the recent stirrings in the village and the whispered rumors of a prophecy, Elara couldn't help but feel that the birthmark was more than just a strange quirk of fate. The warmth she had felt the night before, the glow that had emanated from the mark, all pointed to something greater, something beyond her understanding.

As she sat in her small room, the morning light filtering through the window, Elara stared at the birthmark on her wrist. The symbol was unlike anything she had seen before—an intricate design that seemed to pulse with a life of its own. It was a perfect circle, within which were delicate lines and curves, forming a pattern that was both beautiful and mysterious. It seemed to glow faintly in the morning light, a soft luminescence that made the hairs on the back of her neck stand on end.

She traced the lines of the symbol with her finger, feeling the warmth radiating from it. The sensation was both comforting and unsettling, as if the mark was trying to communicate with her, to tell her something that she could not yet understand.

Elara's thoughts were interrupted by the sound of footsteps approaching her door. She quickly pulled down her sleeve, covering the birthmark, and stood up just as the door creaked open. Liora stepped into the room, her expression a mixture of worry and determination.

"Elara," Liora said, her voice firm. "We need to talk."

Elara nodded, her heart pounding in her chest. She had been waiting for this conversation, knowing that her mother had more to say about the birthmark and the prophecy. But now that the moment had arrived, she felt a wave of apprehension wash over her.

Liora gestured for Elara to sit, and the two of them settled on the edge of the bed. For a moment, neither spoke, the silence heavy with unspoken words. Finally, Liora took a deep breath and began.

"You know that I've always told you to keep your birthmark hidden," Liora said, her voice steady. "And you've done well to follow that advice. But now, with everything that's happening in the village, it's time you knew the truth."

Elara listened intently, her eyes fixed on her mother's face. She could see the tension in Liora's expression, the way her hands fidgeted in her lap, as if she were struggling to find the right words.

"Your father and I... we knew from the moment you were born that you were special," Liora continued, her voice softening. "When we saw the mark on your wrist, we realized that you were connected to something ancient, something powerful. Your father believed that it was a sign, a symbol that linked you to the prophecy."

Elara's heart skipped a beat at the mention of her father. He had died when she was just a baby, and her mother rarely spoke of him. "What did Father think it meant?" Elara asked, her voice barely above a whisper.

Liora sighed, her eyes clouded with memories. "He believed that the mark was a sign from the gods, a symbol that marked you as the chosen one—the one destined to uncover the secrets of the forgotten city."

Elara's mind raced as she processed her mother's words. The chosen one? The prophecy? It was all too much to take in. She had grown up hearing the tales of the forgotten city and the prophecy, but she had never imagined that they could be connected to her.

"But why me?" Elara asked, her voice trembling. "Why was I chosen?"

Liora shook her head, her expression one of sorrow. "I don't know, Elara. Your father and I tried to understand, but we could never find the answers. All we knew was that the mark on your wrist was significant, and that it tied you to the prophecy in ways we couldn't comprehend."

Elara stared at the floor, her thoughts swirling in confusion. She had always known that she was different, but this was beyond anything she could have imagined. The weight of the prophecy, the responsibility it entailed, pressed down on her like a heavy burden.

"But what am I supposed to do?" Elara asked, her voice filled with uncertainty. "How am I supposed to fulfill this prophecy when I don't even know where to start?"

Liora reached out and took Elara's hand, squeezing it gently. "I can't give you all the answers, Elara. But I believe that the mark will guide you, just as it has guided you so far. You have a connection to the forgotten city, a connection that will lead you to the truth. You just have to trust in yourself and in the path that lies ahead."

Elara looked up at her mother, her eyes filled with a mixture of fear and determination. She didn't fully understand what was happening, but she knew that she couldn't ignore the call of the prophecy. Something deep within her, something primal and instinctual, urged her to follow the path that was laid out before her.

"I'll try, Mother," Elara said, her voice resolute. "I'll do whatever it takes to uncover the secrets of the forgotten city."

Liora smiled, though her eyes were filled with tears. "I know you will, my dear. You're stronger than you realize, and I have faith that you'll find the answers you're seeking."

The two of them sat in silence for a moment, the weight of the conversation settling over them like a heavy blanket. Finally, Liora stood up, her expression more composed. "You should get ready for the day," she said, her voice returning to its usual calm tone. "There's still work to be done, and we can't afford to fall behind."

Elara nodded, grateful for the return to normalcy. She needed time to process everything she had learned, and the familiar routine of daily chores would give her the space she needed to think.

As Liora left the room, Elara stood up and walked to the window, gazing out at the village below. The morning sun bathed the rooftops in a warm glow, and the mountains loomed in the distance, their peaks shrouded in mist. Elara's heart ached with a mixture of fear and longing. The mountains were calling to her, just as they had the night before. She knew that her journey was just beginning, and that it would take her far from the safety of her home.

But she also knew that she couldn't turn back now. The prophecy had been set in motion, and she was the one destined to fulfill it. She would uncover the secrets of the forgotten city, no matter what it took.

With a deep breath, Elara turned away from the window and began to prepare for the day. She didn't know what the future held, but she was ready to face it head-on.

The Village Whispers

THE VILLAGE OF DUNCASTER was small, with a population of only a few hundred people. It was the kind of place where everyone knew each other, where secrets were hard to keep, and where rumors spread like wildfire. Elara had grown up here, had known most of the villagers her entire life. She had always felt a sense of belonging, a comfort in the familiarity of her surroundings.

But now, with the revelation of her birthmark and the connection to the prophecy, everything felt different. As she went about her chores that day, she couldn't shake the feeling that the villagers were watching her, their eyes filled with curiosity and suspicion.

It began as she fetched water from the well. A group of women stood nearby, chatting in hushed tones. Elara caught snippets of their conversation as she passed by.

"Did you hear about Elara?" one woman whispered. "They say she's the one from the prophecy."

"The chosen one?" another woman gasped. "But she's just a girl!"

Elara's cheeks flushed with embarrassment as she hurried past them, her heart pounding in her chest. She had always been shy, uncomfortable with attention, and now it seemed that the entire village was focused on her.

The whispers followed her throughout the day. As she helped her mother gather herbs in the forest, she overheard a group of men talking in low voices.

"They say she's marked by the gods," one man said, his voice filled with awe. "A symbol on her wrist, just like in the prophecy."

"But what does it mean?"

another man asked, his tone skeptical. "What's so special about her?"

Elara tried to ignore the whispers, but it was impossible. Everywhere she went, people were talking about her, speculating about her role in the prophecy. The attention made her uneasy, filling her with a sense of dread. She didn't want to be the center of attention, didn't want to be seen as different. But it seemed that her fate had already been decided for her.

By the time the sun began to set, Elara was exhausted, both physically and emotionally. She had spent the day avoiding the curious gazes and whispered conversations, but she couldn't escape the feeling that something had changed. The village no longer felt like the safe, familiar place it had once been. It felt foreign, as if she no longer belonged.

As she made her way back to her cottage, Elara felt a deep sense of unease settle over her. She knew that the villagers meant no harm, that their curiosity was natural given the circumstances. But she couldn't help but feel like an outsider, like she was being pushed into a role she wasn't ready to play.

When she finally reached her home, she found Liora waiting for her in the doorway. Her mother's expression was sympathetic, as if she understood the turmoil Elara was going through.

"Come inside, Elara," Liora said gently. "You've had a long day."

Elara nodded, grateful for the warmth and comfort of her home. She followed her mother inside and sank into a chair by the fire, feeling the tension in her body begin to ease.

Liora busied herself with preparing a simple meal, her movements calm and deliberate. She didn't speak, allowing Elara the space to gather her thoughts. When the meal was ready, they sat down together at the small wooden table, the flickering firelight casting soft shadows on the walls.

As they ate, Elara finally spoke, her voice hesitant. "Mother, do you think the villagers are right? Do you think I'm the one from the prophecy?"

Liora looked at her daughter, her expression thoughtful. "I believe that the mark on your wrist is significant, Elara. It ties you to the prophecy in ways that we don't fully understand. But whether you're truly the chosen one... that's something only time will tell."

Elara nodded, her heart heavy with uncertainty. She wanted to believe that she was destined for something great, that her birthmark was a sign of a higher purpose. But at the same time, she was afraid—afraid of the responsibility, afraid of the unknown.

"I'm scared," Elara admitted, her voice barely above a whisper. "What if I'm not ready for this? What if I fail?"

Liora reached across the table and took Elara's hand, her grip firm and reassuring. "You're stronger than you think, Elara. I know this is overwhelming, but you don't have to face it alone. I'm here for you, and so are the elders. They've spent their lives studying the prophecy, and they can help guide you."

Elara felt a surge of gratitude for her mother's unwavering support. She didn't know what the future held, but she knew that she wouldn't have to face it alone. With her mother by her side, she felt a little more confident, a little more prepared to take on the challenges ahead.

After dinner, Elara went to her room and sat by the window, staring out at the darkened village. The night was quiet, the only sound the gentle rustling of the wind through the trees. The stars twinkled overhead, their light soft and distant, like the promise of something yet to come.

Elara traced the symbol on her wrist, feeling the warmth that still lingered there. The mark was a part of her, a connection to something ancient and powerful. She didn't fully understand it yet, but she knew that it was important—that it would guide her on the path ahead.

As she sat there, lost in thought, a strange sense of calm washed over her. The fears and doubts that had plagued her all day began to fade, replaced by a quiet determination. She didn't know what the future held, but she was ready to face it, whatever it might bring.

The Elders' Council

THE NEXT MORNING, ELARA awoke to find a message waiting for her. It was a simple note, written in neat, careful script, asking her to meet with the village elders at the communal hall. The request was not unexpected—she had known that the elders would want to speak with her after the events of the previous night. But it still filled her with a sense of apprehension.

After dressing and eating a quick breakfast, Elara made her way to the communal hall. The building was one of the oldest in the village, its stone walls weathered and worn by time. It was a place of importance, where the villagers gathered for meetings, celebrations, and ceremonies. It was also where the elders held their council, discussing matters of great significance to the community.

When Elara arrived, she found the elders already gathered inside. They were seated in a semicircle around the large wooden table that dominated the center of the room. Elder Mirela, the oldest and most respected of the group, sat at the head of the table, her sharp eyes focused on Elara as she entered.

"Thank you for coming, Elara," Elder Mirela said, her voice calm and measured. "Please, have a seat."

Elara nodded and took the empty seat at the table, feeling the weight of the elders' gaze upon her. She had known most of them her entire life—Elder Thane, with his deep, resonant voice and stern demeanor; Elder Brynn, with her kind eyes and gentle smile; and Elder Kael, with his sharp mind and quick wit. They were the leaders of the village, the keepers of its history and traditions.

But today, they looked at her with a mixture of curiosity and concern, as if they were seeing her in a new light.

"We've heard the rumors," Elder Mirela began, her voice steady. "The villagers are talking about you, Elara. They believe that you may be the one from the prophecy, the chosen one destined to uncover the secrets of the forgotten city."

Elara swallowed, her mouth suddenly dry. "I... I don't know if I am," she admitted. "But I have the mark—the symbol mentioned in the prophecy. And I've felt... something. A connection to the mountains, to the city. I don't fully understand it, but it's there."

The elders exchanged glances, their expressions thoughtful.

"May we see the mark?" Elder Thane asked, his voice gentle.

Elara hesitated for a moment before nodding. She pulled back her sleeve, revealing the symbol on her wrist. The elders leaned forward, studying the mark with a mixture of awe and reverence.

"It's just as the prophecy described," Elder Brynn murmured, her eyes wide. "An intricate symbol, glowing with an inner light."

Elder Kael nodded, his expression serious. "There's no doubt that this mark is significant. It ties you to the prophecy in ways we don't fully understand. But what does it mean? What is your role in all of this?"

Elara shook her head, her frustration bubbling to the surface. "I don't know," she said, her voice tinged with desperation. "I wish I had answers, but I don't. All I know is that I feel this... pull, this connection to the mountains. It's like they're calling to me, urging me to find the forgotten city."

Elder Mirela leaned back in her chair, her expression thoughtful. "The prophecy speaks of a chosen one who will unlock the mysteries of the forgotten city and restore its knowledge to the world. But it also speaks of trials, of challenges that the chosen one must overcome. The path ahead will not be easy, Elara."

Elara nodded, her heart heavy with the weight of the prophecy. "I understand. But I'm willing to do whatever it takes. I want to uncover the truth, to find out what the prophecy really means."

The elders exchanged glances once more, their expressions solemn.

"Then you must begin your journey," Elder Mirela said, her voice firm. "The path will be difficult, and you will face many challenges. But we believe in you, Elara. You are stronger than you realize, and you have the support of the entire village."

Elder Thane nodded in agreement. "We will provide you with whatever resources you need. Supplies, guidance, anything that will help you on your journey."

Elder Brynn smiled warmly at Elara. "And remember, you are not alone. We are with you, every step of the way."

Elara felt a surge of gratitude for the elders' support. She had feared that they might doubt her, that they might dismiss the prophecy as nothing more than a legend. But instead, they believed in her, believed that she could fulfill the prophecy and uncover the secrets of the forgotten city.

"I'm ready," Elara said, her voice filled with determination. "I'll do whatever it takes to fulfill the prophecy and uncover the truth."

Elder Mirela smiled, her expression one of pride and affection. "We know you will, Elara. You are destined for greatness."

The meeting continued for some time, with the elders discussing the details of Elara's journey. They provided her with a map of the mountains, marking the locations of ancient ruins and hidden paths that might lead her to the forgotten city. They also gave her a small pouch of supplies—dried food, a flask of water, and a few simple tools that would help her survive in the wilderness.

As the meeting drew to a close, the elders stood and gathered around Elara, their expressions solemn.

"May the gods guide you on your journey," Elder Mirela said, her voice filled with reverence. "And may you find the answers you seek."

Elara nodded, her heart filled with a mixture of fear and determination. She didn't know what the future held, but she was ready to face it. The prophecy had set her on a path, and she would follow it, no matter where it led.

With the support of the elders and the villagers, Elara felt a newfound sense of purpose. She was the chosen one, marked by destiny to uncover the secrets of the forgotten city. And she would do whatever it took to fulfill that destiny.

The Call of the Mountains

AS ELARA LEFT THE COMMUNAL hall and made her way back to her cottage, she couldn't shake the feeling of anticipation that had settled over her. The elders' words echoed in her mind, filling her with a sense of purpose and determination.

She was the chosen one, destined to uncover the secrets of the forgotten city. It was a responsibility that weighed heavily on her, but it was also a calling that she couldn't ignore.

The mountains loomed in the distance, their peaks shrouded in mist. They seemed to beckon to her, calling her to uncover the mysteries that lay hidden within their depths.

Elara knew that she couldn't delay any longer. The prophecy had set her on a path, and she had to follow it, no matter where it led.

With a deep breath, Elara began to prepare for her journey. She packed her supplies carefully, making sure to include the map and the tools that the elders had given her. She wrapped her cloak tightly around her shoulders, bracing herself for the cold that awaited her in the mountains.

As she prepared to leave, Liora came to her side, her expression filled with a mixture of pride and sorrow.

"You're really going, aren't you?" Liora asked, her voice trembling.

Elara nodded, her heart heavy with the weight of her decision. "I have to, Mother. The prophecy... it's calling to me. I can't ignore it."

Liora sighed, her eyes filled with tears. "I know, Elara. I've known this day would come for a long time. But it doesn't make it any easier."

Elara wrapped her arms around her mother, holding her tightly. "I'll come back, Mother. I promise."

Liora nodded, her voice choked with emotion. "I know you will, my dear. You're strong, and I have faith that you'll find the answers you're seeking."

They stood there for a moment, holding each other, neither wanting to let go. But finally, Elara pulled away, her resolve firm.

"I have to go," Elara said, her voice filled with determination. "The mountains are calling to me, and I can't ignore them."

Liora nodded, her eyes filled with tears. "Go, Elara. And may the gods protect you."

With a final embrace, Elara turned and left the cottage, her heart heavy but her resolve strong. She knew that she was leaving behind everything she had ever known, but she also knew that she was following her destiny.

As she made her way through the village, the villagers watched her with a mixture of awe and reverence. They knew of the prophecy, knew that Elara was the chosen one, destined to uncover the secrets of the forgotten city.

Elara felt their eyes on her, felt the weight of their expectations. But she didn't let it deter her. She was the marked one, the chosen one, and she would fulfill the prophecy, no matter what it took.

As she reached the edge of the village, Elara paused and looked back one last time. The village of Duncaster, her home for her entire life, seemed small and distant now, a place of safety and comfort that she was leaving behind.

But as she turned to face the mountains, she felt a surge of excitement and anticipation. The path ahead was unknown, filled with danger and uncertainty. But it was also filled with possibility, with the promise of uncovering the secrets of the forgotten city.

With a deep breath, Elara began her journey, her heart filled with determination and hope. The mountains called to her, and she would answer that call, no matter where it led.

Chapter 3: The Call to Adventure

The Vision

Night had fallen over the village of Duncaster, and Elara lay in her bed, her mind buzzing with the events of the past few days. The revelation of her birthmark, the whispers of the prophecy, and the weight of being the chosen one had left her feeling both exhilarated and overwhelmed. She had spent the day preparing for her journey, gathering supplies and saying her goodbyes to the villagers who had come to wish her well. But now, as she lay in the darkness, the reality of what lay ahead began to sink in.

The mountains loomed large in her mind, their peaks shrouded in mist and mystery. She had always felt a connection to the mountains, but now that connection felt stronger than ever. It was as if they were calling to her, urging her to uncover their secrets and fulfill the prophecy that had been set in motion long before she was born.

As she drifted off to sleep, her thoughts swirled with images of the forgotten city, of ancient ruins and hidden paths. The weight of the prophecy pressed down on her, filling her dreams with a sense of urgency and purpose. But amidst the chaos of her thoughts, a vision began to take shape—one that would guide her on the path to her destiny.

In her dream, Elara found herself standing at the edge of a vast, mist-shrouded forest. The trees were tall and ancient, their branches twisted and gnarled as if they had been shaped by the passage of time. The air was thick with the scent of pine and earth, and the only sound was the rustling of leaves in the gentle breeze.

Elara felt a sense of familiarity as she gazed into the depths of the forest, as if she had been here before. But she knew that this place was not real, at least not in the waking world. It was a vision, a dream sent to her by forces beyond her understanding.

As she took a step forward, the mist began to part, revealing a narrow path that wound its way through the trees. The path was overgrown and faint, as if it had not been traveled in many years. But there was a pull, a force that urged her to follow it, to see where it led.

Elara hesitated for a moment, her heart pounding in her chest. She knew that this path was important, that it was tied to the prophecy and the forgotten city. But there was also a sense of danger, a feeling that once she set foot on this path, there would be no turning back.

With a deep breath, Elara stepped onto the path, her feet crunching on the fallen leaves. The forest closed in around her, the trees towering overhead and casting long shadows on the ground. The air was thick with an otherworldly energy, and Elara could feel the presence of something ancient and powerful watching over her.

As she walked, the path began to change. The trees became taller and more imposing, their branches forming a canopy that blocked out the sky. The air grew colder, and the mist thickened, swirling around her like a living thing. But despite the growing sense of unease, Elara pressed on, driven by a force she could not explain.

Finally, after what felt like hours of walking, Elara reached a clearing in the forest. In the center of the clearing stood a massive stone archway, its surface covered in intricate carvings that seemed to glow with a faint, ethereal light. The archway was ancient, older than anything Elara had ever seen, and it radiated a sense of power and mystery.

Elara stepped closer to the archway, her heart pounding with a mixture of fear and excitement. She could feel the energy emanating from the stone, could hear a faint humming that seemed to vibrate in her bones. It was as if the archway was alive, pulsing with the same energy that had guided her to this place.

As she reached out to touch the stone, the carvings on the archway began to glow brighter, their light filling the clearing with a soft, golden radiance. The humming grew louder, filling her ears with a sound that was both beautiful and terrifying.

And then, just as suddenly as it had begun, the light dimmed, and the humming faded away. Elara stood there, her hand still pressed against the stone, her heart racing with the intensity of the vision.

But before she could fully comprehend what had happened, the archway began to shift and change. The carvings on its surface moved and twisted, forming new patterns and symbols that seemed to dance before her eyes. And then, as if guided by an invisible hand, the stone in the center of the archway began to shimmer and ripple, like the surface of a pond disturbed by a stone.

Elara watched in awe as the shimmering stone transformed into a portal—a gateway to another place, another world. Through the portal, she could see a landscape unlike anything she had ever known—a vast expanse of rolling hills and ancient ruins, bathed in the golden light of a setting sun.

It was the forgotten city.

Elara's breath caught in her throat as she gazed through the portal, her mind reeling with the realization that she had found the path to the city. This was the place she had seen in her dreams, the place that the prophecy had foretold. And now, it was within her reach.

But as she took a step toward the portal, a voice echoed through the clearing, deep and resonant, yet gentle and soothing.

"Elara," the voice called, sending a shiver down her spine. "The time has come. You must find the forgotten city and uncover its secrets. But beware, for the path is fraught with danger. Only the chosen one can succeed, but you must be prepared for the trials that lie ahead."

Elara looked around, searching for the source of the voice, but there was no one there. The clearing was empty, save for the ancient archway and the portal that shimmered within it.

But the voice continued, filling the clearing with its otherworldly presence. "Follow the path, Elara. Seek the hermit who awaits you at the edge of the forest. He will guide you on your journey and provide you with the tools you need to succeed. But remember, the journey will be perilous, and you must trust in yourself and in the mark that you bear."

Elara felt a surge of determination as the voice spoke, filling her with a sense of purpose and resolve. She knew that this was her destiny, that she was the one destined to fulfill the prophecy. And now, the path to the forgotten city was clear.

With a final glance at the portal, Elara turned and began to walk back down the path, the vision fading as she moved further away from the archway. The forest closed in around her once more, the mist thickening and the shadows growing longer. But despite the growing darkness, Elara felt a sense of calm and certainty. She knew what she had to do.

The vision began to fade, the images of the forest and the archway dissolving into darkness. But the voice echoed in her mind, a final reminder of the task that lay ahead.

"Find the hermit, Elara. He will guide you on your journey. And remember, the path to the forgotten city is one of trials and challenges. But you are the chosen one, and you will succeed."

And with those final words, the vision faded completely, and Elara was plunged into darkness.

The Awakening

ELARA AWOKE WITH A start, her heart pounding in her chest and her mind racing with the intensity of the vision. She sat up in bed, her breath coming in ragged gasps as she tried to make sense of what she had seen.

The vision had been so vivid, so real. She could still feel the cold air of the forest, could still see the glowing carvings on the ancient archway. And the voice—the voice had spoken to her with a clarity that left no doubt in her mind. This was no ordinary dream; it was a message, a call to action.

Elara looked down at her wrist, at the symbol that had been with her since birth. The mark was glowing faintly, just as it had in the vision, a reminder of the destiny that awaited her.

She knew what she had to do.

With a newfound sense of purpose, Elara rose from her bed and began to prepare for her journey. The vision had shown her the path, had guided her to the edge of the forest where the hermit awaited. She didn't know who this hermit was or how he would help her, but she trusted in the vision, in the voice that had spoken to her.

As she dressed, her mind raced with thoughts of the trials that lay ahead. The voice had warned her that the journey would be perilous, that she would face challenges that would test her strength and resolve. But she was ready. She had been chosen to fulfill the prophecy, and she would not falter.

Elara gathered her belongings—her cloak, her satchel of supplies, and the map that the elders had given her. She wrapped her wrist with a cloth to cover the mark, knowing that it was still important to keep it hidden from prying eyes. The villagers meant well, but she couldn't afford any distractions or delays.

As she prepared to leave, she paused for a moment to look around her room. It was small and simple, with a wooden bed, a chest for her clothes, and a small window that overlooked the village. This had been her home for her entire life, the place where she had grown up and felt safe. But now, it felt like a place she was leaving behind, a chapter of her life that was coming to an end.

Elara took a deep breath, steeling herself for what was to come. The vision had set her on a path, and she had to follow it, no matter where it led.

With one last glance around the room, Elara picked up her satchel and made her way to the door. The sun was just beginning to rise, casting a soft golden light over the village. The air was cool and crisp, filled with the scent of morning dew and the sound of birdsong.

Elara stepped outside, her heart heavy with the knowledge that she was leaving her village behind. But she knew that this was the right thing to do, that she had been chosen to fulfill a destiny that was greater than herself.

As she made her way through the village, she noticed that the streets were quiet, the villagers still asleep in their homes. The only sound was the soft crunch of her boots on the dirt path and the distant rustling of leaves in the breeze.

Elara felt a pang of sadness as she passed by the familiar cottages and shops, the places she had known her entire life. But she also felt a sense of excitement, a thrill at the thought of what lay ahead. The vision had shown her the path to the forgotten city, and she was ready to follow it.

As she reached the edge of the village, Elara paused for a moment to look back. The village of Duncaster, with its thatched roofs and stone walls, was bathed in the golden light of dawn, a place of peace and safety. But it was also a place of the past, a place that she was leaving behind as she embarked on her journey.

With a deep breath, Elara turned and faced the mountains. The path ahead was unknown, filled with danger and uncertainty. But it was also filled with possibility, with the promise of uncovering the secrets of the forgotten city.

And so, with her heart full of determination and her mind focused on the task ahead, Elara began her journey into the unknown.

The Hermit

THE PATH THROUGH THE forest was just as Elara had seen it in her vision—narrow, overgrown, and winding through ancient trees that towered overhead. The air was thick with the scent of pine and earth, and the ground was soft beneath her boots, covered in a layer of fallen leaves.

As she walked, Elara couldn't help but feel a sense of déjà vu, as if she had traveled this path before. The vision had been so vivid, so real, that it felt like she was retracing her steps, following a path that had already been laid out for her.

The forest was quiet, save for the occasional rustling of leaves or the distant call of a bird. But there was an undercurrent of energy, a feeling that the forest was alive, watching her as she made her way deeper into its depths.

Elara walked for what felt like hours, the path growing narrower and more treacherous as she went. The trees closed in around her, their branches forming a canopy that blocked out the sky. The air grew colder, and the mist thickened, swirling around her like a living thing.

But despite the growing sense of unease, Elara pressed on, driven by the memory of the vision and the knowledge that the hermit awaited her at the edge of the forest.

Finally, after what felt like an eternity, Elara reached a small clearing in the forest. The mist parted, revealing a small, weathered cottage nestled among the trees. The cottage was old, its wooden walls worn and covered in moss, its roof sagging under the weight of years. But there was a sense of warmth and safety emanating from the cottage, a feeling that this was a place of refuge.

Elara approached the cottage, her heart pounding with a mixture of fear and anticipation. She didn't know what to expect, didn't know who this hermit was or how he would help her. But she trusted in the vision, in the voice that had guided her here.

As she reached the door, Elara hesitated for a moment, her hand hovering over the worn wooden handle. She could feel the energy radiating from the cottage, a sense of ancient power that filled her with both awe and trepidation.

Taking a deep breath, Elara knocked on the door, the sound echoing through the clearing.

For a moment, there was silence, and Elara wondered if she had come to the wrong place. But then, she heard the sound of footsteps from within the cottage, followed by the creak of the door as it slowly opened.

Standing in the doorway was an old man, his face lined with age and wisdom. His hair was long and silver, his beard thick and unkempt. He wore a simple robe, made of coarse, homespun fabric, and his eyes were a deep, piercing blue that seemed to see right through her.

Elara felt a shiver run down her spine as she met the man's gaze. There was something about him, something otherworldly and powerful, that made her feel both small and insignificant.

"Elara," the old man said, his voice deep and resonant. "I've been expecting you."

Elara's eyes widened in surprise. "You know who I am?"

The old man nodded, a faint smile tugging at the corners of his lips. "I know many things, child. I know of the mark you bear, of the prophecy that has been set in motion. And I know that you are the one destined to uncover the secrets of the forgotten city."

Elara's heart raced as she listened to the old man's words. "How do you know all of this?"

The old man stepped aside, gesturing for Elara to enter the cottage. "Come inside, and I will explain everything."

Elara hesitated for a moment, her mind racing with questions and doubts. But she knew that she had no choice—this was the path that had been laid out for her, and she had to follow it.

With a deep breath, Elara stepped into the cottage, the door creaking shut behind her.

The interior of the cottage was simple and rustic, with a small hearth, a wooden table, and a few shelves lined with books and jars of herbs. The air was warm and fragrant, filled with the scent of burning wood and dried flowers.

The old man gestured for Elara to sit at the table, and she did so, feeling a sense of calm settle over her as she took in her surroundings.

The old man took a seat across from her, his piercing blue eyes never leaving her face. "You are wondering who I am," he said, his voice soft and gentle.

Elara nodded, her heart pounding in her chest. "Yes. And how you know so much about me."

The old man smiled, a twinkle of amusement in his eyes. "I am known as the Hermit of the Blackstone Mountains. I have lived here for many years, watching and waiting for the one who would fulfill the prophecy."

Elara's mind raced as she tried to process his words. "You've been waiting for me?"

The Hermit nodded, his expression serious. "Yes. The prophecy has been passed down through the generations, and I have been entrusted with the knowledge of it. I have watched over the mountains, waiting for the chosen one to appear."

Elara felt a sense of awe and responsibility settle over her. "And you believe that I'm the chosen one?"

The Hermit's gaze softened, and he reached across the table to gently touch the cloth that covered her wrist. "Show me the mark."

Elara hesitated for a moment before slowly unwrapping the cloth and revealing the symbol on her wrist. The Hermit's eyes widened as he saw the mark, and he let out a low whistle of amazement.

"It's just as the prophecy foretold," the Hermit murmured, his voice filled with reverence. "The mark of the chosen one, the symbol of destiny."

Elara stared at the mark, her heart heavy with the weight of her role in the prophecy. "But what does it mean? What am I supposed to do?"

The Hermit's expression grew serious, and he leaned back in his chair, his eyes never leaving hers. "The mark is a sign, a connection to the ancient powers that once ruled these lands. It ties you to the forgotten city, to the knowledge and secrets that have been lost to time."

Elara listened intently, her mind racing with questions. "But how do I find the city? The vision showed me a path, but I don't know where to start."

The Hermit nodded, a faint smile tugging at the corners of his lips. "The vision has guided you here, to me. And now, it is my turn to guide you."

He reached into the folds of his robe and pulled out a small, weathered scroll. He carefully unrolled it, revealing an ancient map covered in intricate symbols and markings.

"This is the map to the forgotten city," the Hermit explained, his voice filled with reverence. "It has been passed down through the generations, entrusted to those who guard the secrets of the prophecy. It will guide you on your journey, showing you the hidden paths and ancient ruins that lead to the city."

Elara's eyes widened as she gazed at the map, her heart pounding with excitement and anticipation. "This... this is the key to finding the city."

The Hermit nodded, his expression serious. "Yes. But the journey will not be easy, Elara. The path is fraught with danger, and you will face trials that will test your strength, your courage, and your resolve."

Elara felt a surge of determination as she listened to the Hermit's words. "I'm ready," she said, her voice filled with resolve. "I'll do whatever it takes to fulfill the prophecy and uncover the secrets of the forgotten city."

The Hermit smiled, a twinkle of pride in his eyes. "I have no doubt that you will succeed, Elara. You have been chosen for this task, and the mark on your wrist is proof of that."

He handed her the map, his expression serious. "But remember, Elara, the journey will be perilous. You must trust in yourself, in the mark that you bear, and in the guidance of the ancient powers."

Elara took the map, her hands trembling with a mixture of fear and excitement. "I will," she promised, her voice steady. "I won't let you down."

The Hermit nodded, his expression filled with pride and affection. "I know you won't, Elara. You are the chosen one, and you will fulfill the prophecy."

As Elara prepared to leave, the Hermit placed a hand on her shoulder, his eyes filled with a deep, ancient wisdom. "May the gods protect you on your journey, Elara. And may you find the answers you seek."

Elara nodded, her heart full of determination and resolve. She knew that the path ahead would be difficult, but she was ready to face whatever challenges lay in her way.

With the map in hand and the Hermit's words ringing in her ears, Elara stepped out of the cottage and into the forest. The sun was beginning to set, casting long shadows on the ground and bathing the trees in a warm, golden light.

As she made her way down the path, Elara felt a sense of calm and certainty settle over her. She knew what she had to do, and she was ready to face the trials that lay ahead.

The journey had begun, and there was no turning back.

The Perilous Journey

THE FOREST WAS QUIET as Elara made her way down the narrow path, the map clutched tightly in her hand. The trees loomed overhead, their branches forming a canopy that blocked out the sky. The air was thick with the scent of pine and earth, and the ground was soft beneath her boots, covered in a layer of fallen leaves.

Elara's mind raced with thoughts of the journey ahead. The Hermit's words echoed in her ears, filling her with a sense of urgency and purpose. The path to the forgotten city was fraught with danger, but she was ready to face whatever challenges lay in her way.

As she walked, Elara couldn't shake the feeling that she was being watched. The forest was alive with an otherworldly energy, and she could feel the presence of something ancient and powerful lurking in the shadows.

But she pressed on, driven by the memory of the vision and the knowledge that she was the chosen one, destined to fulfill the prophecy.

The path grew narrower and more treacherous as she went, the trees closing in around her and the air growing colder. The mist thickened, swirling around her like a living thing, obscuring her vision and making it difficult to see more than a few feet ahead.

Elara kept her eyes on the map, her heart pounding with a mixture of fear and determination. The map showed her the way, guiding her through the twists and turns of the forest and leading her closer to the forgotten city.

But the journey was not without its dangers.

As she made her way deeper into the forest, Elara encountered a series of obstacles that tested her strength and resolve. The path was blocked by fallen trees and tangled roots, forcing her to climb and crawl her way through the underbrush. The air grew colder, and the mist thickened, making it difficult to see and breathe.

But Elara refused to give up. She knew that this was the path that had been laid out for her, and she was determined to see it through to the end.

As the sun began to set, casting long shadows on the ground, Elara reached a steep, rocky incline that led up to the edge of a cliff. The map showed that this was the final obstacle before reaching the forgotten city, and Elara knew that she had to climb it if she wanted to fulfill the prophecy.

Taking a deep breath, Elara began to climb, her hands and feet finding purchase on the rough, uneven rocks. The climb was difficult, the rocks slick with moisture and the air thin and cold. But Elara pressed on, driven by the memory of the vision and the knowledge that she was the chosen one.

As she reached the top of the cliff, Elara paused to catch her breath, her heart pounding in her chest. The view from the top was breathtaking, with the forest stretching out before her and the mountains rising in the distance.

But there was no time to admire the view. The forgotten city lay ahead, hidden in the depths of the mountains, and Elara knew that she had to keep moving.

With the map in hand and the Hermit's words ringing in her ears, Elara began her descent down the other side of the cliff, the path growing steeper and more treacherous as she went.

The air grew colder, and the mist thickened, making it difficult to see and breathe. But Elara pressed on, driven by the memory of the vision and the knowledge that she was the chosen one.

As she made her way down the rocky incline, Elara couldn't shake the feeling that she was being watched. The forest was alive with an otherworldly energy, and she could feel the presence of something ancient and powerful lurking in the shadows.

But she refused to give in to fear. She was the chosen one, destined to fulfill the prophecy and uncover the secrets of the forgotten city.

Finally, after what felt like hours of climbing, Elara reached the bottom of the incline and found herself standing at the entrance to a narrow, winding path that led into the mountains.

The path was overgrown and faint, as if it had not been traveled in many years. But there was a pull, a force that urged her to follow it, to see where it led.

Elara took a deep breath, steeling herself for the journey ahead. The forgotten city was within her reach, and she was ready to face whatever challenges lay in her way.

With the map in hand and the Hermit's words ringing in her ears, Elara stepped onto the path and began her journey into the unknown. The mountains loomed large before her, their peaks shrouded in mist and mystery. The air was cold and thin, filled with the scent of pine and earth.

But Elara pressed on, driven by the memory of the vision and the knowledge that she was the chosen one, destined to fulfill the prophecy and uncover the secrets of the forgotten city.

The journey was long and perilous, but Elara was ready. She had been chosen for this task, and she would see it through to the end, no matter what it took.

As she made her way deeper into the mountains, Elara couldn't shake the feeling that she was being watched. The air was thick with an otherworldly energy, and she could feel the presence of something ancient and powerful lurking in the shadows.

But she refused to give in to fear. She was the chosen one, destined to fulfill the prophecy and uncover the secrets of the forgotten city.

And with that thought in mind, Elara pressed on, her heart filled with determination and resolve. The journey had begun, and there was no turning back.

Chapter 4: The Guardian of the Mountain Pass

The Mountain Pass

The air grew colder and thinner as Elara ascended the steep, rocky path that led to the mountain pass. The sun was beginning to dip behind the peaks, casting long shadows over the rugged landscape. The higher she climbed, the more treacherous the path became, with loose stones shifting under her feet and jagged rocks jutting out from the mountainside. Each step required careful balance and unwavering focus, but Elara pressed on, driven by the knowledge that the forgotten city was within her reach.

The map the Hermit had given her was clutched tightly in her hand, its ancient parchment worn and fragile. The path it revealed was one that few had ever taken, and even fewer had survived. But Elara was determined. The prophecy had set her on this course, and she would not falter now.

As she climbed, Elara couldn't shake the feeling that she was being watched. The air was thick with an otherworldly energy, and the silence of the mountains was almost deafening. There were no birds, no animals, no sound at all except for the crunch of gravel underfoot and the occasional gust of wind that howled through the peaks. It was as if the mountain itself was holding its breath, waiting for something.

The path grew steeper still, winding its way up the side of the mountain in a series of sharp switchbacks. The incline was so steep that Elara had to use her hands to steady herself, gripping the rough stone as she pulled herself up the incline. Her muscles burned with the effort, and her breath came in ragged gasps, but she refused to slow down. The mountain pass was close now—she could feel it.

Finally, after what felt like hours of grueling ascent, Elara reached a narrow ledge that jutted out from the side of the mountain. The ledge was barely wide enough for her to stand on, and below her, the ground dropped away into a dizzying chasm. She paused for a moment, catching her breath and taking in the view. The entire valley lay spread out beneath her, bathed in the golden light of the setting sun. It was a breathtaking sight, but Elara had no time to admire it. The pass was just ahead, and with it, the final challenge that stood between her and the forgotten city.

Elara turned her attention back to the path and saw that it led to a narrow opening in the mountainside, just wide enough for a person to pass through. The opening was framed by two massive stone pillars, each one carved with intricate designs that had been worn smooth by centuries of wind and rain. The passageway beyond the pillars was dark and foreboding, the light of the setting sun barely penetrating its depths.

Elara knew that this was the entrance to the mountain pass, the final obstacle before reaching the forgotten city. But as she stepped closer to the pillars, a deep, rumbling sound echoed through the mountains, vibrating the very ground beneath her feet.

She froze, her heart pounding in her chest, as the rumbling grew louder, shaking the stone pillars and sending small rocks tumbling down the mountainside. The sound was like thunder, deep and resonant, but it wasn't coming from the sky—it was coming from within the mountain itself.

Elara's breath caught in her throat as she realized what was happening. The guardian of the mountain pass had awakened.

The Stone Golem

THE RUMBLING GREW LOUDER, and Elara watched in awe and fear as the stone pillars began to shift and move. The intricate carvings that adorned the pillars glowed with a faint, ethereal light, and the stone seemed to come alive, shifting and rearranging itself into new shapes. The ground beneath Elara's feet trembled as the pillars transformed before her eyes, merging together to form a massive figure that loomed over the entrance to the pass.

The figure was a golem, a giant made entirely of stone. Its body was composed of the same rough, weathered rock as the mountainside, and its eyes glowed with a fiery red light. The golem stood at least twenty feet tall, its massive limbs moving with a slow, deliberate grace that belied its immense size. It was a creature of ancient power, a guardian that had stood watch over the mountain pass for centuries, perhaps even millennia.

Elara felt a shiver of fear run down her spine as the golem turned its gaze toward her, its glowing eyes fixing on her with an intensity that made her feel as if it could see straight into her soul. The golem's presence was overwhelming, its sheer size and power filling the narrow ledge with an aura of ancient, elemental force.

For a moment, Elara was frozen in place, her mind racing as she tried to figure out what to do. The golem was clearly the guardian of the pass, and it would not allow her to proceed without a challenge. But how could she, a mere human, hope to defeat such a creature?

The golem took a step forward, its massive foot causing the ground to shake beneath Elara's feet. It raised one of its stone arms, and Elara braced herself for the impact, her heart pounding in her chest. But instead of striking, the golem spoke, its voice deep and resonant, like the rumble of distant thunder.

"Who dares to enter the mountain pass?" the golem intoned, its voice echoing off the walls of the mountainside. "Who dares to challenge the guardian of the forgotten city?"

Elara swallowed hard, her throat dry with fear, but she forced herself to speak. "I am Elara, the one chosen by the prophecy. I seek the forgotten city to uncover its secrets and fulfill my destiny."

The golem regarded her in silence for a moment, its glowing eyes narrowing as it studied her. Then, with a slow, deliberate movement, it lowered its arm and stepped back, allowing Elara to approach.

"You seek the forgotten city," the golem rumbled, its voice filled with ancient wisdom. "But to pass through this gate, you must first prove yourself worthy. You must answer the riddle of the guardian."

Elara felt a surge of relief that the golem was not going to attack her outright, but her heart still pounded with anxiety. A riddle—this was a test of her wits, not her strength. She had always been clever, quick to solve problems and puzzles, but this was different. The stakes were higher than they had ever been.

"Ask your riddle, Guardian," Elara said, trying to keep her voice steady.

The golem's eyes glowed brighter, and the air around them seemed to hum with energy as it prepared to speak.

The Riddle of the Guardian

THE GOLEM'S VOICE WAS deep and resonant as it began to speak, each word vibrating in the air like the tolling of a great bell.

"I am not alive, yet I grow. I do not breathe, yet I flow. I have no voice, yet I roar. What am I?"

Elara's mind raced as she considered the riddle. It was a classic riddle, one that required her to think beyond the literal meaning of the words and find the deeper connection between them. She repeated the riddle in her mind, dissecting each line as she searched for the answer.

"I am not alive, yet I grow."

The first line suggested something that was inanimate, yet had the ability to increase in size or change over time. Elara thought of plants, of trees, but they were alive. Perhaps it was something else—something that grew but was not considered a living being.

"I do not breathe, yet I flow."

The second line pointed her toward water—rivers and streams that flowed without the need for breath. But water didn't grow, did it? Or perhaps it did, in a way. A river could swell, expand, grow in volume after a storm or during the spring thaw. But it wasn't just water, was it?

"I have no voice, yet I roar."

The third line made the connection clear. Water—specifically, a river. A river didn't have a voice, but it roared as it crashed over rocks and waterfalls, as it surged and swelled with power.

Elara's eyes lit up as she realized the answer. "A river," she said aloud, her voice filled with confidence. "The answer is a river."

The golem's eyes flashed with light, and for a moment, Elara feared that she had answered incorrectly. But then the golem's massive head nodded slowly, and its voice rumbled through the air like the sound of boulders tumbling down a mountainside.

"You have answered correctly, Elara," the golem intoned, its voice filled with a note of approval. "A river is indeed the answer to the riddle. You have proven your wit and your worthiness."

Elara let out a breath she hadn't realized she was holding, relief flooding through her. She had solved the riddle, had proven herself to the guardian. But the golem wasn't finished yet.

"You have passed the first trial," the golem said, its voice growing softer, more contemplative. "But there is one more challenge that you must face before I can allow you to pass."

Elara's heart sank as she heard the golem's words. She had hoped that solving the riddle would be enough, but it seemed that there was more to the guardian's test than she had anticipated.

"What is the second challenge?" Elara asked, her voice steady despite the anxiety that gnawed at her.

The golem was silent for a moment, as if considering its response. Then, with a slow, deliberate movement, it raised one of its massive stone hands and extended it toward Elara. In

its palm was a small, glowing orb of light, no larger than a marble.

"This is the Heart of the Mountain," the golem explained, its voice filled with reverence. "It is the source of my power, the essence of the mountains themselves. To pass through the gate, you must take this orb and carry it with you on your journey. But beware—for as long as you carry it, the Heart of the Mountain will test you. It will weigh on your soul, challenging your resolve and your strength. Only if you can bear its weight will you be worthy to enter the forgotten city."

Elara stared at the glowing orb in the golem's hand, her heart pounding with a mixture of fear and awe. The Heart of the Mountain—this was no ordinary test. It was a test of her very soul, a challenge that would push her to her limits and beyond.

But Elara knew that she had no choice. The prophecy had set her on this path, and she would see it through, no matter what it took.

"I will take the Heart of the Mountain," Elara said, her voice filled with determination. "I will carry it with me and prove my worthiness."

The golem's eyes glowed brighter, and for a moment, the air around them seemed to hum with energy. Then, with a slow, deliberate movement, the golem lowered its hand and placed the glowing orb in Elara's palm.

The moment the orb touched her skin, Elara felt a surge of energy course through her body. It was like nothing she had ever felt before—an intense, almost overwhelming force that seemed to vibrate in her very bones. The orb was warm to the touch, and it pulsed with a steady, rhythmic beat, like the heartbeat of the mountain itself.

Elara clenched her fist around the orb, her breath coming in short, sharp gasps as she tried to steady herself. The weight of the orb was not physical, but it was heavy nonetheless, pressing down on her soul with a force that threatened to crush her.

But Elara refused to give in. She had been chosen to fulfill the prophecy, and she would not falter now. With a deep breath, she steadied herself and looked up at the golem, her eyes filled with resolve.

"I am ready," Elara said, her voice strong and steady. "I will carry the Heart of the Mountain and face whatever challenges lie ahead."

The golem's eyes glowed with approval, and it stepped back, allowing Elara to pass through the gate. The entrance to the mountain pass loomed before her, dark and foreboding, but Elara felt no fear. She had proven herself to the guardian, had taken up the challenge of the Heart of the Mountain, and now, the path to the forgotten city was clear.

With the glowing orb clutched tightly in her hand, Elara stepped forward, crossing the threshold and entering the mountain pass.

The Weight of the Heart

THE MOUNTAIN PASS WAS narrow and winding, the path barely wide enough for Elara to walk. The walls of the pass were steep and jagged, rising up on either side like the jaws of some great beast. The air was cold and thin, and the only sound was the crunch of gravel underfoot and the distant howl of the wind as it whipped through the peaks.

Elara could feel the weight of the Heart of the Mountain pressing down on her soul with every step she took. It was a heavy burden, one that threatened to overwhelm her, but she refused to give in. She had taken up the challenge, and she would see it through, no matter what it took.

As she made her way through the pass, Elara's thoughts were filled with memories of her journey so far. She thought of the Hermit, of the vision that had guided her to the path, of the village she had left behind. She thought of the prophecy and the weight of the destiny that had been placed upon her shoulders.

But most of all, she thought of the forgotten city—the place that had been lost to time, the place that held the answers she sought. It was within her reach now, just beyond the mountain pass, and Elara knew that she was closer than ever to fulfilling her destiny.

But the journey was far from over.

As Elara continued to walk, the weight of the Heart of the Mountain grew heavier, pressing down on her with a force that made it difficult to breathe. Her steps grew slower, more labored, and the air around her seemed to thicken, making it difficult to see.

The path ahead was shrouded in darkness, and Elara felt a surge of panic rise in her chest as she realized that she could no longer see the way forward. The walls of the pass seemed to close in around her, the jagged rocks looming overhead like the teeth of a great beast.

But Elara refused to give in to fear. She clenched her fist around the glowing orb, feeling its warmth seep into her skin, and took a deep breath. The path was still there, she knew it was—she just had to keep moving forward.

Step by step, Elara pressed on, her breath coming in ragged gasps as she fought against the weight of the Heart of the Mountain. The darkness pressed in around her, but she could feel the orb's warmth guiding her, leading her forward through the shadows.

The air grew colder still, and Elara's limbs felt heavy and sluggish, as if they were weighed down by invisible chains. Her thoughts grew muddled, her vision blurred, but she forced herself to keep moving, driven by the knowledge that the forgotten city was just beyond the pass.

Finally, after what felt like an eternity, Elara saw a faint light ahead—just a small, flickering glow, barely visible through the darkness. It was the end of the pass, the gateway to the forgotten city.

With the last of her strength, Elara pushed forward, her heart pounding with a mixture of fear and determination. The light grew brighter as she approached, and the darkness began to lift, revealing the path ahead.

Elara stumbled forward, her limbs trembling with exhaustion, and finally emerged from the mountain pass. The walls of the pass fell away, and she found herself standing on a narrow ledge overlooking a vast, mist-shrouded valley.

The valley was bathed in the soft, golden light of the setting sun, and in the distance, Elara could see the faint outline of ancient ruins, half-hidden by the mist. It was the forgotten city.

Elara's heart swelled with a mixture of awe and relief as she gazed at the ruins, the place that had been lost to time, the place that held the answers she sought. She had made it through the mountain pass, had proven herself to the guardian, and now, the forgotten city was within her reach.

But the journey was far from over.

The Guardian's Blessing

AS ELARA STOOD ON THE ledge, gazing out at the forgotten city, she felt a presence behind her—a familiar, ancient presence that filled the air with a sense of power and reverence.

She turned to see the stone golem standing at the entrance to the mountain pass, its massive form outlined by the golden light of the setting sun. The golem's eyes glowed with a soft, warm light, and its expression was one of approval and respect.

"You have passed the trials, Elara," the golem rumbled, its voice deep and resonant. "You have proven your wit, your strength, and your resolve. You are worthy to enter the forgotten city."

Elara felt a surge of pride and relief as she listened to the golem's words. She had faced the guardian's challenges and had emerged victorious. But the golem wasn't finished yet.

"You have carried the Heart of the Mountain with you on your journey," the golem continued, its voice filled with reverence. "You have borne its weight and have proven yourself worthy of its power."

Elara looked down at the glowing orb in her hand, feeling its warmth pulsing in her palm. The weight that had pressed down on her soul was gone, replaced by a sense of lightness and clarity. The Heart of the Mountain had tested her, had pushed her to her limits, but she had passed the test.

"You may keep the Heart of the Mountain," the golem said, its voice filled with approval. "It will serve as a guide on your journey, a source of strength and wisdom. But remember, Elara, the journey is not yet over. The forgotten city holds many secrets, and you will face challenges greater than any you have faced so far. But you are the chosen one, and I have no doubt that you will succeed."

Elara nodded, her heart filled with determination and resolve. She had come this far, and she would see the journey through to the end, no matter what it took.

"Thank you, Guardian," Elara said, her voice filled with gratitude. "I will not forget your wisdom, nor the challenges you set before me."

The golem's eyes glowed brighter, and it bowed its massive head in a gesture of respect. "May the gods protect you on your journey, Elara. And may you find the answers you seek."

With those final words, the golem turned and stepped back into the mountain pass, its massive form dissolving into the shadows as it returned to its place of rest.

Elara watched as the golem disappeared from view, her heart filled with a mixture of awe and respect. The guardian had tested her, had pushed her to her limits, but she had emerged victorious. And now, the path to the forgotten city was clear.

With the Heart of the Mountain clutched tightly in her hand, Elara turned and faced the valley below. The ancient ruins of the forgotten city were half-hidden by the mist, but she could see them clearly now, a place of mystery and power that held the answers she sought.

The journey was not yet over, but Elara was ready. She had proven herself to the guardian, had taken up the challenge of the Heart of the Mountain, and now, the path to the forgotten city lay before her.

With a deep breath, Elara began her descent into the valley, her heart filled with determination and resolve. The forgotten city was within her reach, and she would uncover its secrets, no matter what it took.

The sun was setting behind the mountains, casting long shadows over the valley, but Elara felt no fear. She had faced the trials of the guardian, had proven herself worthy, and now, she was ready to face whatever challenges lay ahead.

The journey had begun, and there was no turning back.

Chapter 5: The Enchanted Forest

The Entrance to the Forest

Elara descended from the mountain pass with the Heart of the Mountain clutched tightly in her hand, the valley before her bathed in the soft, fading light of dusk. The forgotten city lay somewhere beyond the horizon, hidden within the mists that clung to the ancient trees like a shroud. Her journey had been long and perilous, but she knew that the greatest challenges still lay ahead.

As she approached the edge of the valley, the landscape began to change. The rocky terrain of the mountains gave way to dense, lush greenery, and the air grew thick with the scent of pine and damp earth. Towering trees with twisted, gnarled trunks loomed over her, their branches forming a canopy so thick that it blocked out the fading sunlight. It was as if she had entered another world—a place where time flowed differently and magic lingered in the air.

This was the Enchanted Forest, a place spoken of in whispers and half-remembered tales, a place where the boundaries between the natural and the supernatural were blurred. Elara had heard the stories, but she had never imagined that she would one day set foot in the forest herself. Now, as she stood at its threshold, she felt a mixture of awe and trepidation.

The trees seemed to bend and sway as if they were alive, their leaves rustling with a sound that was almost like whispers. The air was filled with a faint, otherworldly glow, and Elara could see small, flickering lights dancing among the branches—fireflies, or perhaps something else entirely. She took a deep breath, steeling herself for whatever lay ahead, and stepped into the forest.

The moment she crossed the threshold, the atmosphere changed. The air grew cooler, and the light dimmed further, casting long, shifting shadows on the ground. The trees seemed to close in around her, their trunks twisting and contorting as if they were watching her with unseen eyes. The whispers grew louder, filling her ears with a chorus of soft, unintelligible voices.

Elara pressed on, her footsteps silent on the soft, moss-covered ground. She had the sense that she was being watched, but when she looked around, she saw nothing but the endless rows of trees, their branches swaying gently in the breeze. The forest was alive with magic, and she knew that she would have to be cautious if she hoped to navigate its labyrinthine paths.

As she walked, she felt the weight of the Heart of the Mountain in her hand, its warmth pulsing steadily against her skin. The orb had guided her through the mountain pass, and she hoped that it would continue to guide her through the forest. But as she ventured deeper into the woods, she realized that the Heart's glow was beginning to fade, its light dimming as if it were being smothered by the thick, enchanted air.

Elara's heart raced as the light of the Heart of the Mountain grew fainter. She couldn't afford to lose her way, not now, when she was so close to the forgotten city. She had to find a guide, someone or something that could help her navigate the forest and reach her destination.

Just as the last of the Heart's light flickered out, leaving her in near-total darkness, Elara heard a soft rustling sound behind her. She froze, her senses on high alert, as the sound grew closer. It was the sound of something moving through the underbrush—something small and quick, but with a strange, almost otherworldly quality to its movements.

Elara turned slowly, her hand instinctively going to the hilt of her dagger, though she wasn't sure what good it would do against the magical creatures that might inhabit the forest. As she peered into the shadows, she saw a pair of glowing eyes staring back at her from the darkness. The eyes were bright and curious, their gaze fixed on her with an intensity that made her shiver.

The creature stepped out of the shadows, revealing itself to be a fox—a sleek, red-furred fox with a bushy tail and a sharp, inquisitive expression. But this was no ordinary fox. Elara could see that its fur shimmered with an ethereal light, and its eyes glowed with a wisdom that was far beyond that of any mere animal.

The fox tilted its head to the side, regarding Elara with an expression that was almost amused. Then, to Elara's astonishment, it spoke.

"Well, well," the fox said, its voice soft and melodious, with a hint of mischief. "What do we have here? A human, lost in the Enchanted Forest. You must be very brave or very foolish to venture this far."

Elara's jaw dropped in surprise. She had heard of talking animals in fairy tales and legends, but she had never imagined that she would encounter one herself. For a moment, she was at a loss for words, unsure of how to respond.

The fox chuckled, a sound that was surprisingly warm and friendly. "No need to be so shocked, my dear. You're not the first traveler to stumble into these woods, and you certainly won't be the last. But I must say, it's been quite some time since I've seen a human with such determination in their eyes. Tell me, what brings you to the Enchanted Forest?"

Elara took a deep breath, gathering her composure. "I'm on a journey to find the forgotten city," she explained. "I've been chosen to fulfill a prophecy, and I believe the answers I seek are hidden within the city's ruins. But I've lost my way in the forest, and I don't know how to find the path forward."

The fox's eyes gleamed with interest. "The forgotten city, you say? That's quite the ambitious quest for a lone traveler. But you're in luck, my dear, for I happen to know these woods better than anyone. If it's guidance you seek, I can help you—though I must warn you, the path ahead is fraught with dangers, both seen and unseen."

Elara felt a surge of hope at the fox's words. She had found a guide, someone who could help her navigate the forest and reach the forgotten city. But she was also wary. The forest was a place of magic and mystery, and she couldn't afford to be too trusting.

"Why would you help me?" Elara asked, her voice tinged with suspicion. "What do you gain from guiding me through the forest?"

The fox grinned, baring its sharp, white teeth. "Ah, a cautious one, I see. That's good—it means you're less likely to fall prey to the forest's tricks. As for why I would help you, let's just say I have a vested interest in the success of your journey. The forgotten city holds many secrets, and some of those secrets are tied to this very forest. If you succeed in your quest, it could mean great things for both the city and the forest."

Elara considered the fox's words carefully. There was something about the creature that she found both trustworthy and enigmatic, as if it held knowledge that went far beyond her understanding. She knew that she couldn't afford to refuse its help, but she also couldn't afford to be too trusting.

"All right," Elara said finally. "I'll accept your help. But know this—I'm not afraid to defend myself if it turns out that you have other intentions."

The fox's grin widened, and it dipped its head in a gesture of respect. "Fair enough, my dear. You'll find that I'm a fox of my word. Now, let's not waste any more time. The night is young, and we have a long journey ahead of us."

With that, the fox turned and began to trot down the path, its bushy tail flicking back and forth as it moved. Elara hesitated for a moment, then followed, her senses alert and her hand resting on the hilt of her dagger.

As they ventured deeper into the forest, Elara couldn't shake the feeling that she had just made a pact with a creature far more powerful and knowledgeable than she could ever imagine. But she also knew that she had little choice. The Enchanted Forest was a place of mystery and danger, and she would need all the help she could get if she hoped to reach the forgotten city.

The Forest's Secrets

THE ENCHANTED FOREST was unlike any place Elara had ever seen. The trees towered above her, their trunks so wide that she could scarcely see around them, and their branches formed a dense canopy that blocked out the sky. The air was filled with a soft, glowing light that seemed to come from the forest itself, casting everything in a gentle, otherworldly radiance.

As they walked, Elara noticed that the forest was alive with activity. Small, glowing creatures flitted among the branches, their wings shimmering like diamonds in the dim light. Strange plants with iridescent leaves grew along the path, their tendrils reaching out as if to touch her as she passed by. And all the while, the trees whispered in voices that seemed to come from the very heart of the forest, speaking in a language that Elara couldn't understand.

The fox trotted ahead of her, moving with a grace and ease that suggested it had spent its entire life in the forest. Every so often, it would glance back at Elara, as if to make sure she was still following, and then continue on its way. It seemed to know exactly where it was going, weaving through the trees and avoiding the many pitfalls and traps that lay hidden beneath the forest floor.

As they walked, Elara's curiosity got the better of her, and she decided to ask the fox about the forest and its connection to the forgotten city.

"You mentioned that the secrets of the forgotten city are tied to this forest," Elara said, her voice barely above a whisper. "What did you mean by that?"

The fox glanced back at her, its eyes gleaming with a mixture of amusement and wisdom. "Ah, you're a curious one, aren't you? That's good—curiosity is the key to unlocking the secrets of this world. But I must warn you, some secrets are better left buried."

Elara frowned, sensing that the fox was avoiding her question. "I need to know," she insisted. "If I'm going to fulfill the prophecy, I need to understand the connection between the city and the forest."

The fox sighed, a sound that was surprisingly human, and slowed its pace so that it was walking beside Elara. "Very well," it said. "I suppose you have the right to know, given the journey you've undertaken. But understand that what I'm about to tell you is not just a story—it's a history, one that has been forgotten by most but remembered by the spirits of this forest."

Elara listened intently as the fox began to speak, its voice low and melodic, as if it were reciting a tale that had been passed down through generations.

"Long ago, before the forgotten city was lost to time, it was the heart of a great civilization—a place of knowledge, power, and magic. The people of the city were wise and learned, their minds filled with the secrets of the universe. They built grand temples and libraries, filled with scrolls and tomes that held the knowledge of the ages."

"But with great knowledge came great hubris. The people of the city believed that they could control the forces of nature, that they could bend the will of the gods to their own desires. They sought to unlock the secrets of immortality, to become like the gods themselves."

Elara felt a shiver run down her spine as she listened to the fox's words. She had heard stories of civilizations that had fallen due to their arrogance, but this felt different—more immediate, more personal.

"Their quest for power led them to the forest," the fox continued. "This forest has always been a place of magic, a place where the boundaries between the natural and the supernatural blur. The people of the city sought to harness the magic of the forest, to use it to achieve their own ends. But they did not understand the consequences of their actions."

Elara's heart pounded in her chest as she realized where the story was leading. "What happened?" she asked, her voice barely above a whisper.

The fox's eyes darkened, and its voice grew somber. "The magic of the forest is ancient and powerful, but it is also unpredictable. The people of the city disturbed the balance, and in doing so, they unleashed forces that they could not control. The forest itself turned against them, its magic becoming wild and untamed. The spirits of the forest—the guardians of its secrets—rose up to protect it, but it was too late. The city was consumed by the very forces it had sought to control."

Elara felt a deep sense of sorrow and fear as she listened to the fox's tale. The forgotten city had not simply been lost to time—it had been destroyed, its people consumed by their own arrogance and greed. And now, the forest was all that remained, its magic still potent and dangerous.

"The spirits of the city's former inhabitants now dwell within the forest," the fox said, its voice filled with a note of sadness. "They guard the knowledge and treasures that were lost when the city fell, but they are also wary of those who seek to uncover them. The forest is a place of both wonder and danger, and only those who are truly worthy can unlock its secrets."

Elara's mind raced as she tried to process everything she had just heard. The forest was not just a place of magic—it was a graveyard, a place where the spirits of the past lingered, guarding the knowledge that had once been the pride of a great civilization. And now, she was walking among those spirits, seeking the very knowledge that had led to the city's downfall.

"But why would the prophecy lead me here?" Elara asked, her voice filled with uncertainty. "If the knowledge of the city is so dangerous, why am I being guided to it?"

The fox looked at her with a gaze that was both knowing and compassionate. "Because the knowledge of the city is not inherently evil," it said. "It is the way in which it was used that led to the city's destruction. The prophecy speaks of a chosen one who will uncover the secrets of the city and use them to restore balance, to heal the wounds that were inflicted by the hubris of the past. You are that chosen one, Elara, and it is your task to ensure that the knowledge you uncover is used wisely."

Elara felt a heavy weight settle on her shoulders as she realized the true nature of her quest. She was not just seeking the forgotten city for her own sake—she was seeking it to restore balance, to right the wrongs of the past. It was a task that filled her with both fear and determination, but she knew that she could not turn back now.

"Thank you for telling me," Elara said softly. "I will do my best to fulfill the prophecy and use the knowledge I find wisely."

The fox nodded, its expression one of approval. "I have no doubt that you will, my dear. But remember, the path ahead is fraught with danger. The spirits of the forest will test you, and you must prove yourself worthy before they will allow you to pass."

Elara nodded, her resolve firm. She had faced challenges before, and she was prepared to face whatever tests the forest had in store for her. With the fox as her guide, she felt more confident in her ability to navigate the enchanted woods and reach the forgotten city.

The Spirits of the Forest

AS THEY CONTINUED THEIR journey through the forest, the atmosphere around them grew even more mystical. The trees seemed to whisper more urgently, their voices rising and falling in a rhythmic cadence that was almost like a chant. The air grew thicker, and the glowing lights that flitted among the branches became brighter, casting eerie shadows on the forest floor.

Elara felt a growing sense of unease as they walked, as if the very ground beneath her feet was alive with energy. The fox had warned her that the spirits of the forest would test her, and she could feel their presence all around her—watching, waiting, assessing her every move.

Finally, after what felt like hours of walking, the fox came to a stop in a small clearing. The trees here were even larger and more ancient, their trunks twisted and gnarled, and their branches reaching up to the sky like the arms of giants. The air was thick with magic, and Elara could feel a powerful presence all around her, as if the very forest itself was holding its breath.

"This is the heart of the forest," the fox said, its voice low and reverent. "It is here that the spirits of the city's former inhabitants dwell, guarding the knowledge and treasures that were lost when the city fell. You must prove yourself worthy before they will allow you to pass."

Elara's heart pounded in her chest as she looked around the clearing, her senses alert for any sign of the spirits. She knew that this was a test, and she would need all of her wits and courage to succeed.

As she stood in the clearing, the whispers of the trees grew louder, rising to a crescendo that echoed through the forest like the roar of a great wind. The ground beneath her feet began to tremble, and the air grew heavy with the weight of unseen eyes.

Then, without warning, the trees themselves began to move. Their branches twisted and contorted, and their trunks groaned and creaked as they shifted and rearranged themselves. The clearing seemed to come alive, the very ground pulsing with energy as the spirits of the forest began to manifest.

Elara watched in awe and fear as the spirits took shape before her eyes. They were ethereal, ghostly figures, their forms flickering like shadows in the dim light. Some were humanoid, their features vague and indistinct, while others were more animalistic, their bodies shifting and changing like smoke. They moved with a grace that was both beautiful and terrifying, their eyes glowing with a light that was both ancient and wise.

The spirits circled around Elara, their voices rising in a chorus of whispers that filled her ears with a sound that was both haunting and mesmerizing. She could feel their power, their magic, pressing down on her like a great weight, and she knew that she was being judged.

The fox stepped forward, its fur bristling with energy as it addressed the spirits. "She is the chosen one," it said, its voice strong and clear. "She has come to fulfill the prophecy and restore balance. I vouch for her worthiness."

The spirits' whispers grew louder, and Elara felt a wave of uncertainty wash over her. She knew that this was her moment of judgment, and she had to prove herself worthy of their trust.

Taking a deep breath, Elara stepped forward, her voice trembling but determined. "I am Elara, the one chosen by the prophecy. I seek the forgotten city to uncover its secrets and use them to restore balance. I know that the knowledge I seek is dangerous, but I promise to use it wisely, to ensure that the mistakes of the past are not repeated."

The spirits continued to circle around her, their eyes fixed on her with an intensity that made her feel as if they could see straight into her soul. The pressure of their gaze was almost overwhelming, but Elara refused to back down. She knew that this was her test, and she would face it with all the strength and courage she could muster.

For what felt like an eternity, the spirits assessed her, their whispers rising and falling in a rhythmic cadence that seemed to echo in the very depths of her mind. Elara could feel their power, their ancient wisdom, pressing down on her, but she stood her ground, her resolve unwavering.

Finally, after what felt like hours, the spirits' whispers began to die down, and the pressure of their gaze lessened. The ethereal figures began to retreat, their forms fading back into the shadows of the trees, until only one remained—a tall, regal figure with eyes that glowed like the light of a thousand stars.

The spirit stepped forward, its gaze fixed on Elara with an intensity that made her heart race. When it spoke, its voice was deep and resonant, filled with a wisdom that was beyond human comprehension.

"You have proven yourself worthy, Elara," the spirit said, its voice echoing through the clearing like the tolling of a great bell. "You have shown courage, determination, and a willingness to learn from the mistakes of the past. The knowledge you seek is dangerous, but it is also necessary. You may pass, and may the gods guide your journey."

Elara felt a wave of relief wash over her as the spirit's words echoed in her mind. She had passed the test, had proven herself to the spirits of the forest, and now, the path to the forgotten city was clear.

The spirit's form began to fade, its light dimming as it retreated back into the shadows of the trees. The other spirits followed suit, their ethereal forms dissolving into the darkness until the clearing was once again silent and still.

Elara stood alone in the heart of the forest, her heart pounding with a mixture of fear and exhilaration. She had faced the spirits of the forest and had emerged victorious. But she knew that her journey was far from over.

The fox trotted up to her side, its eyes filled with pride and approval. "You've done well, Elara," it said, its voice warm and encouraging. "The spirits have granted you passage, but remember—the knowledge you seek is both powerful and dangerous. Use it wisely, and you will succeed in your quest."

Elara nodded, her resolve firm. She had come this far, and she would see the journey through to the end, no matter what it took.

"Thank you for your guidance," Elara said softly. "I couldn't have done it without you."

The fox grinned, its eyes gleaming with mischief. "Oh, I'm sure you could have managed on your own, but I'm glad to have been of service. Now, come—there is still much to do, and the forgotten city awaits."

With that, the fox turned and began to lead the way out of the clearing, its bushy tail flicking back and forth as it moved. Elara followed, her heart filled with a mixture of determination and anticipation.

As they ventured deeper into the forest, the atmosphere around them began to change. The trees grew taller and more majestic, their trunks straight and strong, and the air grew lighter, filled with the scent of flowers and fresh earth. The whispers of the trees grew softer, more melodic, as if the forest itself was guiding her toward her destination.

Finally, after what felt like hours of walking, they reached the edge of the forest. The trees parted, revealing a vast, open landscape bathed in the golden light of the setting sun. In the distance, Elara could see the ruins of the forgotten city, half-hidden by the mist but still visible against the backdrop of the mountains.

Elara's heart swelled with a mixture of awe and excitement as she gazed at the ruins. The forgotten city—her destination, the place that held the answers she sought—was within her reach.

The fox turned to her, its eyes gleaming with a mixture of pride and encouragement. "You've made it this far, Elara. The forgotten city lies ahead, but remember—your journey is far from over. The trials you've faced so far are nothing compared to what awaits you within the city's walls. But I have faith in you. You are the chosen one, and you will succeed."

Elara nodded, her resolve firm. She had faced the challenges of the Enchanted Forest, had proven herself to the spirits, and now, the path to the forgotten city was clear.

With the Heart of the Mountain clutched tightly in her hand and the fox by her side, Elara took a deep breath and began her final approach to the forgotten city. The sun was setting behind the mountains, casting long shadows over the landscape, but Elara felt no fear. She was the chosen one, destined to fulfill the prophecy, and she would uncover the secrets of the forgotten city, no matter what it took.

The journey had begun, and there was no turning back.

Chapter 6: The River of Time

The Approach to the River

Elara's journey through the Enchanted Forest had been fraught with challenges and revelations, but nothing could have prepared her for what lay ahead. The forest had been a place of secrets and spirits, where the ancient and the mystical intertwined, but now, as she stood at the edge of the clearing, she faced an entirely new and daunting obstacle: the River of Time.

The ruins of the forgotten city were within reach, just beyond the river, their ancient stones glinting in the pale light of the early dawn. The mist that had shrouded them was beginning to lift, revealing the skeletal remains of once-grand structures—temples, towers, and palaces, now crumbling and overgrown with vines. But between Elara and those ruins lay a barrier that was more formidable than any she had faced before: the River of Time.

The river was unlike any she had ever seen. Its waters were not the usual clear blue or murky brown of ordinary rivers; instead, they shimmered with an ethereal glow, a mixture of colors that seemed to shift and change with each passing moment. The surface of the water was smooth and glassy, but beneath that calm facade, Elara could sense a powerful, restless current—a current that did not just move forward, but backward as well, defying the natural order of time.

Elara had heard of the River of Time in the old stories, tales told by the elders around the fire on cold winter nights. It was said that the river was a conduit between the past and the present, a place where the flow of time was fluid and unpredictable. Those who dared to cross it would witness visions of the past, scenes from history that played out like a dream, offering glimpses of what once was and what could have been. But the river was also treacherous, its currents capable of dragging the unwary into the depths of time itself, trapping them in an endless loop of memories and forgotten moments.

As she stood on the riverbank, the fox by her side, Elara felt a shiver of apprehension. She knew that the river was a crucial part of her journey—its waters held the secrets of the forgotten city, the clues she needed to understand its fate and the reason for its disappearance. But she also knew that crossing the river would not be easy. She would have to navigate its currents carefully, deciphering the visions it showed her while avoiding the traps and dangers that lurked beneath the surface.

The fox, sensing her hesitation, looked up at her with its sharp, intelligent eyes. "This is the River of Time," it said, its voice soft but firm. "It is a place of great power and great danger. To cross it, you must be prepared to face the past—both the past of the forgotten city and your own. The river will show you visions, scenes from history that may help you on your journey, but it will also test you. You must remain focused, Elara, and do not let the current sweep you away."

Elara nodded, taking a deep breath to steady her nerves. "I understand," she said, her voice resolute. "I'm ready."

The fox studied her for a moment, as if assessing her resolve, and then nodded in approval. "Very well," it said. "I will guide you to the edge of the river, but from there, you must navigate the waters on your own. Remember what I've told you—stay focused, trust your instincts, and do not let the visions distract you from your goal."

With that, the fox led her to the very edge of the river, where the ground sloped gently down to the water's edge. The air was cool and still, and the only sound was the gentle lapping of the water against the shore. Elara could see her reflection in the river, her face pale and tense, her eyes filled with a mixture of determination and fear.

The fox stopped at the edge of the water and turned to face her. "This is where I leave you, Elara," it said. "The river is your test, and you must face it alone. But know this—I have faith in you. You are the chosen one, destined to uncover the secrets of the forgotten city and restore balance. Trust in yourself, and you will succeed."

Elara felt a surge of gratitude for the fox's guidance and support. "Thank you," she said, her voice filled with sincerity. "I won't forget what you've done for me."

The fox smiled, a warm, mischievous grin that lit up its face. "Go now, Elara," it said. "The River of Time awaits."

Elara took a deep breath, her heart pounding in her chest, and stepped into the water.

The First Vision: The Birth of the City

THE MOMENT ELARA STEPPED into the river, she felt a rush of cold water against her skin, and the world around her seemed to blur and shift. The landscape of the riverbank faded away, replaced by a swirling vortex of colors and light. She was no longer standing on solid ground—instead, she was floating, weightless, in the middle of the river, surrounded by the ever-changing flow of time.

The river's current tugged at her, pulling her in different directions, but Elara focused on keeping her balance, her mind sharp and alert. She could feel the weight of the Heart of the Mountain in her hand, its warmth a steady anchor that kept her grounded amidst the swirling chaos.

As she floated in the river, the water around her began to change, taking on a silvery, reflective quality. It was as if the river had transformed into a giant mirror, reflecting images from the past, scenes that had been lost to time.

The first vision came suddenly, without warning, like a splash of cold water to the face. The silvery surface of the river rippled, and the reflections began to shift and coalesce into a coherent scene. Elara watched, her breath caught in her throat, as the vision unfolded before her eyes.

She was no longer in the river—instead, she found herself standing on a vast, open plain, bathed in the golden light of a setting sun. The air was warm and filled with the scent of blooming flowers and fresh earth. In the distance, she could see a bustling city—a city that was alive with activity and energy, its streets filled with people and its buildings gleaming in the sunlight.

This was the forgotten city, but not as it was now—in ruins and decay. This was the city as it had been in its prime, a place of beauty, prosperity, and power. The people of the city were dressed in fine garments, their faces filled with happiness and contentment as they went about their daily lives. Merchants sold their wares in the marketplace, children played in the streets, and scholars debated in the shade of grand temples.

Elara watched in awe as the vision played out before her. She could see the city's great towers rising up into the sky, their spires gleaming with gold and silver. She could see the grand libraries, filled with scrolls and books, where scholars and sages studied the secrets of the universe. She could see the temples, where priests and priestesses offered prayers to the gods, their voices filled with reverence and devotion.

This was the city as it had been at the height of its power—a place of learning, culture, and wisdom. But even as Elara marveled at the beauty of the vision, she could sense an undercurrent of unease, a tension that lay beneath the surface.

The vision shifted, and Elara found herself standing in a grand hall, its walls lined with marble columns and its ceiling adorned with intricate frescoes. In the center of the hall stood a group of people—men and women dressed in robes of deep purple and gold, their faces stern and serious. They were gathered around a large, ornate table, upon which lay a scroll, its surface covered in ancient symbols and runes.

The people were deep in discussion, their voices low and urgent. Elara couldn't hear what they were saying, but she could sense the gravity of the moment. These were the leaders of the city, the rulers and sages who held the fate of the civilization in their hands.

As she watched, one of the men—a tall, imposing figure with a thick beard and piercing blue eyes—stepped forward and raised his hand, calling for silence. The room grew still, and the man began to speak, his voice filled with authority and conviction.

"We have achieved much," the man said, his voice echoing through the hall. "Our city has prospered, our people have thrived, and our knowledge has expanded beyond the limits of imagination. But there is more to be done. The gods have blessed us with wisdom and power, but we must use that power wisely. We must continue to seek the secrets of the universe, to unlock the mysteries that lie beyond our understanding."

There was a murmur of agreement from the others, but Elara could sense a note of dissent, a feeling of unease that hung in the air like a shadow.

"But what if we go too far?" a woman's voice spoke up, her tone cautious and wary. She was a slender, graceful figure with long, flowing hair and eyes that glimmered with intelligence. "The gods have given us much, but they have also set limits. We must be careful not to overstep those limits, or we risk bringing disaster upon ourselves."

There was a moment of silence, and then another man—this one younger, with a sharp, angular face and a look of determination—spoke up.

"Limits are meant to be pushed," he said, his voice filled with a fiery passion. "We are on the brink of greatness, of discovering the secrets of immortality, of becoming like the gods themselves. We cannot afford to hold back now. We must press forward, no matter the cost."

The tension in the room grew palpable, and Elara could feel the weight of the decision that lay before these leaders. They were standing at a crossroads, a moment in history that would determine the fate of their civilization. The choice they made would either lead to unimaginable glory or catastrophic ruin.

The vision began to fade, the colors and images dissolving into the silvery waters of the river. But the weight of what she had seen lingered in Elara's mind, a sense of foreboding that gnawed at her soul.

She had witnessed the birth of the forgotten city, the moment when its leaders had made a choice that would set them on a path toward either greatness or destruction. It was a choice that had been driven by ambition, by a desire to transcend the limits set by the gods and achieve immortality. But it was also a choice fraught with danger, a choice that would have far-reaching consequences.

As the vision faded completely, Elara found herself once again floating in the River of Time, the current tugging at her, urging her to move forward. She knew that there was more to see, more to learn about the city's fate. The river would show her the truth, but she had to be prepared for whatever it revealed.

Taking a deep breath, Elara steadied herself and allowed the current to carry her forward, deeper into the river's flow.

The Second Vision: The Fall of the City

THE SECOND VISION CAME more slowly, the images taking shape like mist rising from the water. Elara felt herself being pulled through the currents of time, past moments and memories that blurred together like the pages of a book flipped too quickly. She held on tightly to the Heart of the Mountain, its warmth a constant reminder of her purpose.

The swirling colors around her began to coalesce, forming a new scene. This time, the air was thick with tension, and the sky above was dark and stormy, with clouds swirling ominously. The city was still there, but it was different now—its once-grand buildings were cracked and crumbling, and the streets were eerily empty.

Elara found herself standing in the middle of a desolate square, the grand temple that had once dominated the city's skyline now a ruin of toppled pillars and broken stones. The air was heavy with the smell of smoke and ash, and the sound of distant thunder rumbled ominously in the background.

The city had fallen.

The vision shifted again, and Elara was inside a dark, cavernous chamber, deep within the city's heart. The walls were lined with shelves filled with ancient scrolls and tomes, their pages yellowed with age. In the center of the chamber stood a group of people—different from the ones she had seen before. These people were haggard, their faces lined with worry and fear. They were gathered around a large stone pedestal, upon which lay a massive, glowing crystal.

The crystal pulsed with a faint, rhythmic light, casting an eerie glow over the chamber. The people were speaking in hushed tones, their voices filled with desperation and despair.

"It's too late," one of them said, a man with graying hair and hollow eyes. "The balance has been broken. The power we sought to control has turned against us."

"We must find a way to reverse the damage," a woman said, her voice trembling. "The city is crumbling, the magic is unraveling. If we don't act quickly, everything will be lost."

"But how?" another man asked, his voice filled with anguish. "The power we unleashed is beyond our control. We've sealed our own fate."

Elara's heart ached as she listened to their words. These were the remnants of the city's leaders, the ones who had once stood in that grand hall and made the fateful decision to pursue power at all costs. Now, they were reaping the consequences of that choice, watching as their civilization crumbled around them.

As she watched, the vision began to shift again, the colors blurring and swirling as the scene changed. The chamber faded away, replaced by a view of the city from above—a bird's-eye view of the devastation that had befallen it.

The city was in ruins, its once-majestic towers reduced to rubble, its grand libraries and temples lying in heaps of broken stone. The streets were choked with debris, and the air was thick with smoke. The people who had once thrived in the city were gone, their voices silenced, their lives extinguished.

But amidst the destruction, Elara could see something else—something dark and malevolent, lurking in the shadows of the ruins. It was a presence, a force that radiated power and malice, a force that had been unleashed by the city's quest for knowledge and power.

This was the force that had destroyed the city, the force that had turned its own magic against it. It was a force that had once been controlled, harnessed by the city's leaders, but had now broken free, wreaking havoc on everything it touched.

The vision grew darker, the shadows deepening as the malevolent force spread throughout the city. Elara could feel its power, its anger, as it consumed everything in its path, leaving nothing but destruction in its wake.

The city had fallen, its people wiped out, its knowledge lost to time. But the force that had destroyed it still lingered, a dark and dangerous presence that would not be easily defeated.

As the vision faded, Elara felt a deep sense of sorrow and loss. The city had been a place of great knowledge and power, but it had been destroyed by its own ambition. The very force that its leaders had sought to control had turned against them, bringing about their downfall.

But even as she mourned the loss of the city, Elara knew that there was more to the story. The River of Time had shown her the city's rise and fall, but it had not yet revealed the reason for its disappearance—or the importance of its rediscovery.

There was still more to see, more to learn. Elara took a deep breath, steeling herself for whatever the river would show her next. She allowed the current to carry her forward once again, deeper into the flow of time.

The Third Vision: The Hidden Truth

THE THIRD VISION BEGAN to take shape, the swirling colors of the river coalescing into a new scene. This time, Elara found herself standing on the outskirts of the city, looking out over the ruins from a distance. The city was shrouded in mist, its crumbling towers barely visible through the haze.

But there was something different about this vision—something that set it apart from the others. The air was heavy with magic, a palpable energy that seemed to vibrate in the very ground beneath her feet. The city was not just a place of ruins and memories—it was a place of power, a place where the magic that had once fueled its rise and fall still lingered.

As Elara watched, the mist began to lift, revealing a hidden structure—a temple, half-buried in the earth, its entrance concealed by overgrown vines and ancient stones. The temple was different from the others she had seen—it was older, more primal, its architecture unlike anything she had ever encountered.

This was the source of the city's power—the place where its leaders had first discovered the magic that would both elevate and destroy their civilization.

Elara felt a surge of excitement and trepidation as she realized what she was seeing. This was the key to the city's secrets, the place where its knowledge had been hidden away, waiting to be discovered by those who were worthy.

The vision shifted, and Elara found herself standing inside the temple, the air thick with the scent of ancient incense and the sound of distant chanting. The walls were lined with carvings—intricate symbols and runes that glowed with a faint, otherworldly light. In the center of the chamber stood an altar, upon which lay a large, glowing crystal—the same crystal she had seen in the earlier vision.

But this time, the crystal was different. It pulsed with a steady, rhythmic light, casting a warm, golden glow over the chamber. Elara could feel its power, its magic, radiating from within, filling the air with a sense of awe and reverence.

This was the heart of the city's magic—the source of its power and knowledge. But it was also the source of its downfall.

As Elara approached the altar, she noticed something else—something that had been hidden from her in the earlier visions. There was a figure standing beside the altar, a figure cloaked in shadows, its features obscured by the darkness.

The figure was tall and imposing, its presence filling the chamber with an aura of authority and power. Elara could feel the weight of its gaze as it turned to face her, its eyes glowing with an eerie light.

"You seek the truth," the figure said, its voice deep and resonant, echoing through the chamber like the tolling of a great bell. "You seek the knowledge that was lost when the city fell. But be warned—the truth is not always what it seems. The power you seek is dangerous, and it comes with a price."

Elara's heart raced as she listened to the figure's words. She could sense the gravity of the moment, the weight of the decision that lay before her. The knowledge she sought was within her reach, but she knew that it would come at a cost—a cost that she might not be willing to pay.

"What price?" Elara asked, her voice trembling with a mixture of fear and determination.

The figure's eyes glowed brighter, and it stepped forward, its presence filling the chamber with an overwhelming sense of power. "The price is your soul," it said, its voice filled with a terrible, ancient wisdom. "The knowledge you seek will change you—it will test your resolve, your strength, and your very essence. If you are not careful, it will consume you, just as it consumed those who came before you."

Elara felt a chill run down her spine as she realized the full weight of what the figure was saying. The power of the city's magic was immense, but it was also dangerous—dangerous enough to destroy those who sought to control it.

But even as she grappled with the implications of the figure's words, Elara knew that she could not turn back now. She had come too far, had faced too many challenges, to give up now. The prophecy had led her to this point, and she knew that she had to see it through to the end.

"I understand the risks," Elara said, her voice filled with determination. "But I have to do this. The city's knowledge is too important to be lost forever. I will do whatever it takes to uncover the truth and restore balance."

The figure studied her for a moment, its eyes filled with an ancient, inscrutable wisdom. Then, with a slow, deliberate movement, it nodded.

"Very well," it said, its voice filled with a note of approval. "You have chosen your path. But remember—once you have uncovered the truth, there is no turning back. The knowledge you seek will change you, and it will change the world. Use it wisely, Elara, and may the gods guide your journey."

With those final words, the figure stepped back into the shadows, its form dissolving into the darkness as the vision began to fade.

Elara felt a wave of dizziness as the chamber around her dissolved into the swirling colors of the River of Time. The vision was over, and she was once again floating in the river, its currents tugging at her as they carried her forward.

But even as the vision faded, the weight of what she had seen lingered in her mind. The forgotten city had fallen because of its quest for power, its leaders consumed by their own ambition. But the knowledge that had been lost was not gone forever—it was still there, hidden away in the ruins, waiting to be discovered by those who were worthy.

Elara knew that the journey ahead would not be easy. The river had shown her the truth, but it had also shown her the dangers that lay ahead. The knowledge she sought was powerful, but it was also dangerous—dangerous enough to consume her if she was not careful.

But even as she grappled with the implications of what she had seen, Elara knew that she could not turn back now. The prophecy had led her to this point, and she had to see it through to the end. The fate of the forgotten city—and perhaps the world—depended on it.

Taking a deep breath, Elara steadied herself and allowed the current to carry her forward, deeper into the flow of time. The journey was far from over, but she was ready to face whatever challenges lay ahead.

The Crossing

As Elara floated in the River of Time, she felt the weight of the visions pressing down on her, their images and emotions swirling in her mind like the currents of the river itself. The rise and fall of the forgotten city, the hidden truth of its downfall, the warnings of the mysterious figure—each of these scenes had left an indelible mark on her soul, shaping her understanding of the city's fate and the importance of its rediscovery.

But now, as the river's currents began to slow, Elara sensed that the final part of her journey was approaching. The river had shown her the past, but it had not yet shown her the way forward. She knew that she had to cross the river, to navigate its treacherous currents and reach the other side, where the ruins of the forgotten city awaited.

The water around her began to change, taking on a more turbulent quality as the current grew stronger. The once-calm surface of the river was now churning with energy, the currents swirling and eddying in unpredictable patterns. The silvery light of the river was dimming, replaced by a dark, swirling mist that obscured her vision.

Elara tightened her grip on the Heart of the Mountain, its warmth a steady presence in the midst of the chaos. She knew that she had to cross the river, but the path was unclear, and the currents threatened to drag her under.

With a deep breath, Elara focused on the warmth of the Heart of the Mountain, allowing its steady pulse to guide her. She could feel the pull of the current, but she refused to let it overpower her. She had come too far, faced too many challenges, to be defeated now.

As she moved forward, the mist around her began to lift, revealing the swirling currents of the river in all their chaotic glory. The water was dark and churning, filled with eddies and whirlpools that seemed to reach out for her, trying to pull her under. But Elara was determined. She focused on the path ahead, keeping her mind clear and her movements steady.

The river resisted her efforts, the currents growing stronger and more unpredictable as she pressed on. But Elara refused to give up. She moved with purpose, navigating the treacherous waters with a combination of skill and determination.

Finally, after what felt like an eternity, Elara reached the other side of the river. The water began to calm, the currents slowing and the mist lifting completely. The dark, churning water was replaced by a calm, silvery surface, and the ruins of the forgotten city came into view once again.

Elara felt a surge of relief and triumph as she stepped onto the riverbank, her heart pounding with a mixture of exhaustion and exhilaration. She had crossed the River of Time, had navigated its treacherous currents and witnessed its visions, and now, she stood on the threshold of the forgotten city.

The journey had been long and perilous, filled with challenges and revelations, but Elara knew that it was far from over. The ruins of the city lay before her, filled with the secrets and knowledge that had been lost to time. But they were also filled with danger, with the remnants of the power that had once destroyed the city.

Elara took a deep breath, her resolve firm. She had come this far, and she would see the journey through to the end, no matter what it took.

With the Heart of the Mountain clutched tightly in her hand, Elara stepped forward, her heart filled with determination and resolve. The forgotten city awaited, and she was ready to uncover its secrets.

The journey had begun, and there was no turning back.

Chapter 7: The Temple of Forgotten Gods

The Approach to the Temple

Elara stood on the riverbank, her heart still racing from the ordeal of crossing the River of Time. The ancient ruins of the forgotten city loomed before her, their crumbling structures bathed in the soft, golden light of the setting sun. But amidst the ruins, one structure stood out—a massive, imposing edifice that dominated the landscape with its grandeur and majesty. This was the Temple of Forgotten Gods, a place of reverence and power where the ancient deities of the city had once been worshipped.

The temple was unlike any building Elara had ever seen. Its architecture was a blend of styles, with elements of classical design combined with intricate carvings and symbols that spoke of a deep, ancient magic. The walls were made of smooth, polished stone, their surfaces covered in elaborate frescoes depicting scenes of gods and mortals, of battles and rituals, of creation and destruction. Tall columns lined the entrance, their capitals adorned with the images of mythological creatures—griffins, dragons, and phoenixes—each one rendered with exquisite detail.

At the top of the temple's grand staircase stood a pair of massive doors, each one carved with the image of a god in repose, their eyes closed as if they were in a deep, eternal sleep. The doors were made of a dark, heavy wood that seemed to absorb the light, giving them an ominous, almost foreboding presence. Above the doors, an inscription was etched into the stone in an ancient language that Elara could not read, but she could sense the power and significance of the words.

Elara took a deep breath, her eyes fixed on the temple. She knew that this was her next destination, the place where she would face the challenges set before her by the gods. The prophecy had led her to this point, and now, she had to prove herself worthy of the gods' blessings if she hoped to uncover the secrets of the forgotten city.

The fox, which had guided her through the Enchanted Forest and the River of Time, now stood beside her, its sharp eyes fixed on the temple with a mixture of reverence and caution.

"The Temple of Forgotten Gods," the fox said, its voice filled with a deep respect. "This is where the gods of the city once dwelled, where they were worshipped and revered by the people. But that was long ago. The gods have been forgotten, their temple abandoned and neglected. To enter the temple and seek their blessings, you must first prove yourself worthy. Each god will present you with a challenge, a test of your wisdom, strength, and compassion. Only by passing these tests will you gain their favor and their guidance."

Elara felt a shiver run down her spine as she listened to the fox's words. The challenges ahead would not be easy, but she knew that she had no choice. The gods held the key to the city's secrets, and she needed their blessings if she was to fulfill the prophecy.

"I'm ready," Elara said, her voice steady despite the fear that gnawed at her heart. "Tell me what I must do."

The fox nodded, its eyes gleaming with approval. "The temple's doors will open to you once you approach them. Inside, you will find three chambers, each one dedicated to a different god. In each chamber, you will face a challenge—a test of your wisdom, strength, and compassion. You must succeed in all three challenges to gain the gods' favor. If you fail, the temple will reject you, and the gods will turn their backs on you."

Elara took a deep breath, steeling herself for the trials ahead. She knew that the path would be difficult, but she had come too far to turn back now.

"Thank you for your guidance," Elara said, her voice filled with gratitude. "I will do my best to prove myself worthy."

The fox smiled, a warm, encouraging expression that filled Elara with a sense of hope. "I have no doubt that you will succeed," it said. "Remember—trust in yourself, and trust in the wisdom, strength, and compassion that you carry within you. The gods are watching, but they are also waiting to see if you are truly worthy of their blessings."

With those final words, the fox stepped back, allowing Elara to approach the temple alone.

Elara took one last deep breath, her heart pounding with a mixture of fear and determination, and began to climb the grand staircase that led to the temple's entrance. The stone steps were cool and smooth beneath her feet, and as she ascended, she felt a sense of reverence wash over her. This was a place of power, a place where the boundaries between the mortal and the divine were thin and fragile.

As she reached the top of the staircase, Elara paused for a moment, her eyes fixed on the massive doors before her. The gods' images stared down at her, their faces calm and serene, as if they were waiting for her to make the first move.

With a deep breath, Elara stepped forward and placed her hands on the doors. The wood was cool and solid beneath her fingers, but as she pressed her palms against it, she felt a faint warmth, a pulsing energy that seemed to resonate with the very essence of the temple.

The doors began to shift and creak, their massive weight groaning as they slowly swung open, revealing the dark interior of the temple.

Elara hesitated for a moment, her heart pounding in her chest, but then she stepped forward, crossing the threshold and entering the Temple of Forgotten Gods.

The Chamber of Wisdom

THE INTERIOR OF THE temple was vast and dimly lit, the air thick with the scent of incense and ancient stone. The walls were lined with statues of the gods, their forms carved from the same smooth, polished stone as the temple itself. Each statue was a masterpiece of craftsmanship, its details so finely rendered that they seemed almost lifelike, as if the gods themselves were standing in the chamber, watching Elara with their inscrutable eyes.

As she moved deeper into the temple, Elara noticed that the air seemed to grow heavier, as if it were filled with an invisible pressure. The silence was almost oppressive, broken only by the faint echo of her footsteps on the stone floor.

Finally, after what felt like an eternity, Elara reached the first chamber—a large, circular room with a high, domed ceiling. The walls were covered in intricate frescoes depicting scenes of learning and knowledge—scholars studying ancient texts, sages debating philosophical questions, and gods bestowing wisdom upon mortals.

In the center of the chamber stood a tall pedestal, upon which rested a large, ornate book. The book was bound in rich, dark leather, its cover embossed with the image of an owl—a symbol of wisdom and knowledge. The pages of the book were thick and yellowed with age, and as Elara approached, she could see that they were filled with dense, closely written text.

This was the Chamber of Wisdom, a place where the mind and intellect were tested.

Elara stepped forward, her eyes fixed on the book. She knew that this was her first challenge—the test of wisdom. The book held the key to passing the challenge, but she had no idea what form the test would take.

As she reached out to touch the book, the air in the chamber seemed to shift, and the walls around her began to glow with a soft, golden light. The frescoes came to life, the figures moving and speaking in low, murmuring voices that echoed through the chamber like the rustling of leaves.

Elara felt a sense of awe as she watched the frescoes come alive, the scenes of learning and knowledge playing out before her eyes. But even as she marveled at the beauty of the chamber, she knew that the test was about to begin.

The voice of the owl, the symbol of wisdom, filled the chamber, its tone calm and measured. "You seek the blessing of wisdom," the voice said. "But wisdom is not easily gained. It is a journey, a process of learning and understanding. To pass this challenge, you must demonstrate your wisdom by solving a riddle—a riddle that will test your knowledge, your insight, and your ability to see beyond the surface."

Elara felt a surge of anxiety as she listened to the owl's words. A riddle—a test of her intellect and reasoning. She had always prided herself on her ability to think clearly and logically, but she knew that this would not be an ordinary riddle. The gods' challenges were designed to test her to the very limits of her abilities.

"Listen carefully," the owl continued, its voice filled with a deep, ancient wisdom. "Here is the riddle:

I am not a living being, yet I grow and change.

I have no voice, yet I can speak and teach.

I have no eyes, yet I can see the past and the future.

What am I?"

Elara's mind raced as she considered the riddle. The words echoed in her mind, their meaning elusive and difficult to grasp. She repeated the riddle to herself, trying to break it down and analyze each line.

"I am not a living being, yet I grow and change."

The first line suggested something that was inanimate, yet capable of growth and transformation. Elara thought of plants, of trees, but they were living beings. Perhaps it was something else—something that could evolve or develop over time without being alive.

"I have no voice, yet I can speak and teach."

The second line pointed her toward knowledge, toward something that could convey information or lessons without the need for speech. Books, perhaps—books could teach and impart wisdom, but they had no voice.

"I have no eyes, yet I can see the past and the future."

The third line suggested something that could offer insight or understanding, something that could reveal truths about both the past and the future.

As Elara pieced the riddle together, the answer began to take shape in her mind. The object described in the riddle was not alive, but it could grow and change. It had no voice, but it could teach and convey knowledge. It had no eyes, but it could offer insight into the past and future.

"A book," Elara said aloud, her voice filled with certainty. "The answer is a book."

The moment the words left her lips, the chamber seemed to tremble, and the golden light that filled the room grew brighter. The frescoes on the walls glowed with a radiant energy, and the figures within them turned their gaze toward Elara, their expressions filled with approval.

"You have answered wisely," the owl's voice intoned, its tone filled with respect. "A book is indeed the answer to the riddle. It is a vessel of knowledge, a source of wisdom that can grow and change with time. It can speak and teach without a voice, and it can offer insight into the past and the future."

As the owl spoke, the book on the pedestal began to glow with a soft, golden light, its pages turning as if guided by an invisible hand. The text on the pages seemed to shift and change, revealing new words and symbols that Elara had never seen before.

"You have proven your wisdom," the owl continued. "You are worthy of the blessing of wisdom, the first of the gods' gifts. May your mind be sharp, your thoughts clear, and your understanding deep. Take this blessing with you on your journey, and let it guide you to the truth."

The light in the chamber began to fade, and the frescoes returned to their original state, the figures frozen once again in their eternal poses. The book on the pedestal closed, its glow dimming until it was just an ordinary, albeit ancient, tome.

Elara felt a surge of pride and relief as she realized that she had passed the first challenge. The blessing of wisdom was hers, and she could feel its presence in her mind, a clarity of thought that sharpened her understanding and insight.

But even as she savored her victory, Elara knew that the journey was far from over. The Temple of Forgotten Gods held more challenges—tests of her strength and compassion that would push her to her limits.

With a deep breath, Elara turned and made her way out of the Chamber of Wisdom, her heart filled with determination as she prepared to face the next challenge.

The Chamber of Strength

THE SECOND CHAMBER was located deeper within the temple, down a long, narrow corridor that seemed to stretch on endlessly. The walls were lined with more statues of the gods, their expressions stern and unyielding, as if they were watching her every move. The air grew cooler as Elara moved forward, the silence around her broken only by the faint sound of her footsteps echoing off the stone floor.

Finally, she reached the entrance to the Chamber of Strength—a large, rectangular room with high, vaulted ceilings. The walls were adorned with frescoes depicting scenes of battle and conflict, of warriors clashing in epic struggles, of gods and mortals locked in combat. The floor was made of rough, uneven stone, and the air was filled with the scent of sweat and blood.

In the center of the chamber stood a massive statue of a god, his form towering over the room with an aura of immense power and authority. The god was depicted as a muscular, imposing figure, his body clad in armor and his hands gripping a large, double-headed axe. His expression was fierce and determined, his eyes fixed on some distant horizon as if he were preparing to face an enemy in battle.

This was the Chamber of Strength, a place where physical power and endurance were tested.

Elara stepped forward, her eyes fixed on the statue. She knew that this was her next challenge—the test of strength. The god before her was a symbol of power and might, and she would have to prove herself worthy of his blessing by demonstrating her own strength and determination.

As she approached the statue, the air in the chamber seemed to grow heavier, and the walls began to glow with a faint, red light. The frescoes came to life, the scenes of battle and conflict playing out in vivid detail, the sound of clashing weapons and the cries of warriors filling the air.

Elara felt a surge of adrenaline as she watched the frescoes come alive, the scenes of combat igniting a fire within her. She knew that this challenge would not be easy, but she was ready to face whatever the god had in store for her.

The voice of the god, deep and resonant, filled the chamber, its tone filled with authority and power. "You seek the blessing of strength," the voice said. "But strength is not just physical power—it is the will to endure, the determination to overcome obstacles, the courage to face adversity. To pass this challenge, you must demonstrate your strength in all its forms—strength of body, strength of mind, and strength of spirit."

Elara's heart pounded in her chest as she listened to the god's words. She had always prided herself on her physical endurance and determination, but she knew that this challenge would test her in ways she had never experienced before.

"Step forward," the god's voice commanded, "and face the trials of strength."

Elara took a deep breath, her muscles tensing as she prepared herself for the challenge. She stepped forward, her eyes fixed on the statue, her mind focused on the task ahead.

The first trial began without warning. The ground beneath her feet shifted and trembled, and the floor of the chamber cracked open, revealing a deep chasm filled with jagged rocks and swirling mist. A narrow stone bridge extended across the chasm, its surface rough and uneven, with no handrails or support.

Elara knew that she had to cross the bridge, but she also knew that it would take every ounce of her strength and balance to do so. The chasm below was deep and treacherous, and one misstep could mean certain death.

Taking a deep breath, Elara stepped onto the bridge, her feet carefully finding their footing on the uneven surface. The stone was cold and rough beneath her boots, and the wind that howled through the chasm threatened to knock her off balance.

She moved slowly, her muscles tensed with the effort of maintaining her balance. The bridge swayed slightly with each step, the wind pushing against her, but Elara pressed on, her focus unwavering.

Halfway across the bridge, the wind grew stronger, and the stone beneath her feet began to crack and shift. Elara felt a surge of panic as the bridge trembled beneath her, but she forced herself to stay calm. She knew that she could not afford to lose her balance now.

With a final burst of strength, Elara pushed forward, her body leaning into the wind as she crossed the last few feet of the bridge. The moment her feet touched solid ground on the other side, the bridge collapsed behind her, the stones tumbling into the chasm with a deafening roar.

Elara collapsed to her knees, her breath coming in ragged gasps as she realized that she had passed the first trial. Her muscles burned with exhaustion, but she felt a surge of pride and determination. She had proven her physical strength and endurance, but she knew that the challenge was far from over.

The voice of the god filled the chamber once again, its tone filled with approval. "You have passed the first trial," the voice said. "But there is more to strength than physical power. The next trial will test your strength of mind—the ability to think clearly and make difficult decisions under pressure."

As the god spoke, the chamber began to shift and change. The walls moved closer, the ceiling lowered, and the floor beneath Elara's feet began to rise. The chamber was transforming into a labyrinth, its passages narrow and winding, its walls lined with sharp, jagged stones.

Elara knew that she had to navigate the labyrinth, but she also knew that it would take more than physical strength to do so. The labyrinth was a test of her mind, a challenge that would require her to think clearly and make quick decisions in order to find her way out.

Taking a deep breath, Elara stepped into the labyrinth, her eyes scanning the narrow passageways for any sign of a way out. The walls were close and confining, and the air was thick with the scent of damp earth and stone.

As she moved through the labyrinth, Elara encountered numerous obstacles—dead ends, false passages, and traps that threatened to ensnare her. But she remained focused, her mind sharp and alert, her thoughts clear and decisive.

At one point, Elara came to a fork in the passageway, with two paths leading in opposite directions. One path was dark and narrow, its walls lined with sharp, jagged stones that seemed to close in on her. The other path was wider and well-lit, with smooth walls and a clear view of what lay ahead.

Elara hesitated for a moment, her mind racing as she considered her options. The wider path seemed like the safer choice, but she knew that it might also be a trap—a deceptive illusion designed to lure her into a false sense of security.

Trusting her instincts, Elara chose the narrow, darker path, her body tensing as she squeezed through the tight passageway. The stones scraped against her skin, but she pressed on, her mind focused on finding the way out.

After what felt like an eternity, Elara emerged from the labyrinth, her heart pounding with a mixture of relief and triumph. She had passed the second trial, proving her strength of mind and her ability to make difficult decisions under pressure.

The voice of the god filled the chamber once again, its tone filled with admiration. "You have passed the second trial," the voice said. "But there is one final trial—the test of strength of spirit. This trial will challenge your resolve, your courage, and your will to persevere in the face of overwhelming odds."

As the god spoke, the chamber began to change once more. The walls shifted and expanded, and the ceiling rose to reveal a vast, open space. In the center of the chamber stood a towering figure—a massive, hulking beast with muscles like steel and eyes that glowed with a fierce, predatory light.

The beast was a creature of pure strength, its body a mass of rippling muscles and sinew, its claws and fangs sharp and deadly. It was a symbol of raw, primal power, a force that would test Elara's strength of spirit to its very limits.

Elara knew that she could not defeat the beast with physical strength alone. This was a test of her spirit, a challenge that would require her to summon every ounce of courage and resolve she possessed.

The beast let out a deafening roar, its eyes fixed on Elara with a fierce, predatory gaze. It charged at her, its massive form barreling forward with terrifying speed and power.

Elara stood her ground, her heart pounding with fear, but she refused to back down. She knew that this was the final trial, the ultimate test of her strength of spirit. She had to face the beast head-on, to confront her fear and overcome it.

As the beast closed in on her, Elara raised the Heart of the Mountain, its warm, pulsing energy filling her with a sense of strength and determination. She could feel the power of the gods flowing through her, their blessings giving her the courage to stand against the beast.

The moment the beast reached her, Elara stood firm, her body braced for the impact. The beast lunged at her, its claws outstretched, but Elara held her ground, her spirit unyielding.

The beast collided with her, its massive form slamming into her with the force of a thunderstorm. But Elara did not falter. She felt the weight of the beast pressing down on her, but she refused to give in. She summoned every ounce of her strength, every bit of her resolve, and pushed back against the beast with all her might.

The struggle was fierce and brutal, the beast's power overwhelming, but Elara's spirit was unbreakable. She fought with everything she had, her body and soul united in a single, unwavering purpose.

Finally, after what felt like an eternity, the beast began to weaken. Its massive form trembled, its strength waning as Elara's spirit overcame it. With a final, desperate push, Elara threw the beast off her, its massive body crashing to the ground with a thunderous roar.

The beast let out a final, mournful cry, its body dissolving into mist as the chamber filled with a bright, golden light. The voice of the god echoed through the chamber, its tone filled with pride and admiration.

"You have passed the final trial," the voice said. "You have proven your strength of spirit, your courage, and your resolve. You are worthy of the blessing of strength, the second of the gods' gifts. May your body be strong, your mind sharp, and your spirit unyielding. Take this blessing with you on your journey, and let it guide you to the truth."

As the god's voice faded, the golden light in the chamber began to dim, and the chamber returned to its original state. The statue of the god stood silent and still, its fierce gaze now filled with approval.

Elara felt a deep sense of pride and accomplishment as she realized that she had passed the second challenge. The blessing of strength was hers, and she could feel its presence in her body, mind, and spirit—a powerful, unwavering force that would guide her on her journey.

But even as she savored her victory, Elara knew that the journey was not yet over. There was one final chamber, one final challenge that she had to face—the test of compassion.

With a deep breath, Elara turned and made her way out of the Chamber of Strength, her heart filled with determination as she prepared to face the final challenge.

The Chamber of Compassion

THE THIRD AND FINAL chamber was located at the very heart of the temple, down a long, winding corridor that seemed to stretch on endlessly. The walls were lined with statues of the gods, their expressions gentle and kind, as if they were watching over her with a sense of compassion and understanding. The air grew warmer as Elara moved forward, the silence around her filled with a sense of calm and serenity.

Finally, she reached the entrance to the Chamber of Compassion—a large, circular room with a high, domed ceiling. The walls were adorned with frescoes depicting scenes of kindness and empathy, of gods and mortals helping those in need, of healing and comfort. The floor was made of smooth, polished stone, and the air was filled with the scent of flowers and incense.

In the center of the chamber stood a statue of a goddess, her form radiant with an aura of warmth and love. The goddess was depicted as a gentle, nurturing figure, her hands outstretched in a gesture of compassion and understanding. Her expression was serene and kind, her eyes filled with a deep, abiding empathy.

This was the Chamber of Compassion, a place where the heart and soul were tested.

Elara stepped forward, her eyes fixed on the statue. She knew that this was her final challenge—the test of compassion. The goddess before her was a symbol of kindness and empathy, and she would have to prove herself worthy of her blessing by demonstrating her own compassion and understanding.

As she approached the statue, the air in the chamber seemed to grow warmer, and the walls began to glow with a soft, golden light. The frescoes came to life, the scenes of kindness and empathy playing out before her eyes, the sound of gentle voices and soft laughter filling the air.

Elara felt a sense of peace as she watched the frescoes come alive, the scenes of compassion filling her heart with a sense of warmth and love. But even as she marveled at the beauty of the chamber, she knew that the test was about to begin.

The voice of the goddess, gentle and soothing, filled the chamber, its tone filled with love and understanding. "You seek the blessing of compassion," the voice said. "But compassion is not just a feeling—it is an action, a choice to help others, to heal their wounds and ease their pain. To pass this challenge, you must demonstrate your compassion by helping those in need, by showing kindness and empathy in the face of suffering."

Elara felt a surge of emotion as she listened to the goddess's words. Compassion had always been a guiding principle in her life, but she knew that this challenge would test her in ways she had never experienced before.

"Step forward," the goddess's voice commanded, "and face the trials of compassion."

Elara took a deep breath, her heart filled with a sense of love and empathy, and stepped forward, her eyes fixed on the statue of the goddess.

The first trial began without warning. The chamber around her shifted and changed, the walls dissolving into mist as the floor beneath her feet transformed into soft, fertile soil. Elara found herself standing in a lush, green meadow, the air filled with the scent of wildflowers and the sound of birdsong.

But the peace of the meadow was soon shattered by the sound of crying—a soft, plaintive wail that echoed through the air like a mournful lament. Elara turned and saw a small child standing at the edge of the meadow, their face streaked with tears, their eyes filled with fear and sorrow.

The child was lost, their clothes torn and dirty, their face pale and gaunt. They were clutching a small, worn doll to their chest, their tiny hands trembling with fear.

Elara's heart ached as she saw the child's distress. She knew that this was her first trial—the test of her compassion and empathy.

Without hesitation, Elara walked over to the child, her voice soft and soothing as she knelt beside them. "It's okay," she said, her tone filled with kindness. "You're not alone. I'm here to help you."

The child looked up at her, their eyes filled with a mixture of fear and hope. "I'm lost," the child said, their voice trembling. "I don't know where I am. I want to go home."

Elara's heart swelled with compassion as she listened to the child's words. She knew that she had to help them, to ease their fear and comfort their soul.

Taking the child's hand in her own, Elara smiled gently. "I'll help you find your way home," she said, her voice filled with warmth and love. "You're safe with me."

The child nodded, their tears beginning to dry as they clung to Elara's hand. Together, they walked through the meadow, the air around them filled with a sense of peace and comfort.

As they walked, Elara spoke to the child, her voice gentle and reassuring. She told them stories, sang them songs, and listened to their fears and worries, her heart filled with a deep, abiding empathy.

Finally, after what felt like hours, they reached the edge of the meadow, where a small, cozy cottage stood nestled among the trees. The child's face lit up with joy as they saw the cottage, their eyes filled with hope and relief.

"That's my home!" the child exclaimed, their voice filled with happiness.

Elara smiled, her heart filled with a sense of fulfillment. She had passed the first trial, had shown compassion and kindness to a child in need, and had helped them find their way home.

The meadow around them began to dissolve into mist, the cottage and trees fading away as the chamber returned to its original state. The statue of the goddess stood before Elara, its eyes filled with approval and love.

"You have passed the first trial," the goddess's voice said, its tone filled with warmth. "You have shown compassion and empathy to those in need. But there is more to compassion than kindness—it is also the willingness to forgive, to heal the wounds of the heart and soul. The next trial will test your ability to forgive, to show mercy and understanding in the face of pain and suffering."

As the goddess spoke, the chamber began to shift and change once more. The walls dissolved into mist, and the floor beneath Elara's feet transformed into cold, hard stone. She found herself standing in a dark, narrow alley, the air filled with the scent of damp earth and decay.

In the shadows of the alley, Elara saw a figure huddled against the wall, their body curled in on itself as if they were trying to make themselves as small as possible. The figure was a man, his clothes ragged and dirty, his face gaunt and lined with pain.

As Elara approached, the man looked up at her, his eyes filled with a mixture of fear and guilt. "Please," he said, his voice trembling. "Please forgive me. I didn't mean to do it. I was desperate—I had no other choice."

Elara felt a surge of empathy as she listened to the man's words. She could see the pain and guilt etched into his face, the weight of his actions pressing down on him like a heavy burden.

This was her second trial—the test of forgiveness.

Without hesitation, Elara knelt beside the man, her voice gentle and understanding. "It's okay," she said, her tone filled with compassion. "I forgive you. Whatever you did, I can see that you're truly sorry. I can see that you're suffering."

The man looked at her with a mixture of disbelief and hope, his eyes filling with tears. "You...you forgive me?" he asked, his voice choked with emotion.

Elara nodded, her heart filled with a deep, abiding compassion. "Yes," she said softly. "I forgive you. We all make mistakes, and we all deserve a chance to make things right. You have a good heart—I can see that. It's never too late to change, to heal, to find peace."

The man let out a sob, his body trembling as he wept. "Thank you," he whispered, his voice filled with gratitude. "Thank you for your forgiveness."

Elara placed a comforting hand on the man's shoulder, her heart filled with a sense of love and empathy. She knew that she had passed the second trial, had shown forgiveness and mercy to someone in need of healing.

The alley around them began to dissolve into mist, the cold, hard stone fading away as the chamber returned to its original state. The statue of the goddess stood before Elara, its eyes filled with approval and love.

"You have passed the second trial," the goddess's voice said, its tone filled with warmth and pride. "You have shown forgiveness and mercy, healing the wounds of the heart and soul. But there is one final trial—the test of selflessness, the willingness to sacrifice for the good of others. This trial will challenge your compassion in its purest form."

As the goddess spoke, the chamber began to shift and change once more. The walls dissolved into mist, and the floor beneath Elara's feet transformed into soft, fertile soil. She found herself standing in a lush, green meadow, the air filled with the scent of wildflowers and the sound of birdsong.

But this time, the meadow was different. The sky above was dark and stormy, with clouds swirling ominously. The wind howled through the trees, and the air was thick with tension.

In the center of the meadow, Elara saw a group of people huddled together, their faces filled with fear and desperation. They were surrounded by a circle of fire, the flames burning fiercely, trapping them in the center with no way out.

Elara's heart ached as she saw the people's distress. She knew that this was her final trial—the test of selflessness.

Without hesitation, Elara ran toward the circle of fire, her heart filled with a sense of urgency. The flames were hot and fierce, the heat almost unbearable, but she refused to back down.

As she reached the edge of the fire, Elara saw a small gap in the flames, just wide enough for her to squeeze through. But she knew that it would take all her strength and courage to get the people to safety.

Taking a deep breath, Elara plunged into the flames, the heat searing her skin as she pushed through the fire. She reached the people in the center of the circle, her voice filled with determination as she urged them to follow her.

"Come with me!" she shouted over the roar of the flames. "I'll get you out of here!"

The people looked at her with a mixture of fear and hope, their eyes filled with gratitude as they realized that she was there to help them.

One by one, Elara led them through the gap in the flames, her heart pounding with fear but her resolve unyielding. The heat was intense, the flames threatening to engulf them at any moment, but Elara refused to give up.

Finally, after what felt like an eternity, Elara led the last person through the flames, her body trembling with exhaustion as she collapsed to the ground. The fire behind them died down, the flames flickering out as the stormy sky above began to clear.

Elara felt a deep sense of fulfillment as she realized that she had passed the final trial. She had shown selflessness and compassion, risking her own life to save others.

The meadow around them began to dissolve into mist, the stormy sky and the circle of fire fading away as the chamber returned to its original state. The statue of the goddess stood before Elara, its eyes filled with approval and love.

"You have passed the final trial," the goddess's voice said, its tone filled with warmth and pride. "You have shown selflessness and compassion, sacrificing for the good of others. You are worthy of the blessing of compassion, the third of the gods' gifts. May your heart be filled with love, your soul with empathy, and your spirit with kindness. Take this blessing with you on your journey, and let it guide you to the truth."

As the goddess's voice faded, the chamber began to glow with a soft, golden light, filling Elara with a sense of peace and fulfillment. The statue of the goddess seemed to smile, her expression filled with approval and love.

Elara felt a deep sense of pride and accomplishment as she realized that she had passed the final challenge. The blessing of compassion was hers, and she could feel its presence in her heart, a warm, comforting force that would guide her on her journey.

The journey had been long and arduous, filled with challenges and trials that had tested her in ways she had never imagined. But Elara knew that it was not yet over. The Temple of Forgotten Gods had granted her the blessings of wisdom, strength, and compassion, but now she had to use those blessings to uncover the secrets of the forgotten city and fulfill the prophecy.

With a deep breath, Elara turned and made her way out of the Chamber of Compassion, her heart filled with determination as she prepared to face the final leg of her journey.

The gods had blessed her, and she was ready to fulfill her destiny.

Chapter 8: The Labyrinth of Shadows

The Entrance to the Labyrinth

Elara emerged from the Temple of Forgotten Gods, her heart heavy with the weight of the challenges she had faced. The blessings of wisdom, strength, and compassion now coursed through her, but she knew that the journey was far from over. The path ahead was fraught with even greater trials, and she could sense that the next challenge would test her in ways she had never imagined.

As she descended the temple steps, the landscape before her began to change. The once bright and vibrant world around her grew darker, the light of the sun dimming as thick clouds gathered overhead. The air grew colder, and a sense of foreboding settled over the land. In the distance, Elara could see the outline of a vast, sprawling structure—a labyrinth, its high walls shrouded in shadows and mist.

This was the Labyrinth of Shadows, a place of fear and illusion, where the boundaries between reality and nightmare blurred. It was said that those who entered the labyrinth would be forced to confront their deepest fears and darkest secrets, and that only those with the strongest resolve would emerge unscathed.

Elara took a deep breath, her heart pounding with a mixture of fear and determination. The labyrinth was the next step on her journey, the next trial she had to face in order to fulfill the prophecy. But as she stood at the entrance, staring into the dark, twisting passageways that lay ahead, she couldn't shake the feeling that this challenge would be the most difficult yet.

The blessings of the gods had given her strength, but they had also revealed the weight of the responsibility she carried. The labyrinth would test not only her physical abilities but her very soul—her resolve, her courage, and her ability to confront the darkness within herself.

The entrance to the labyrinth was a massive archway carved from black stone, its surface etched with intricate designs that seemed to pulse with a faint, otherworldly light. The air around the entrance was thick with a palpable sense of dread, as if the very shadows that clung to the walls were alive, waiting to ensnare any who dared to enter.

Elara hesitated for a moment, her mind racing with thoughts of what might await her inside. But she knew that there was no turning back now. The labyrinth was a necessary trial, one that she had to face if she hoped to uncover the secrets of the forgotten city and fulfill her destiny.

With a deep breath, Elara stepped forward, crossing the threshold and entering the Labyrinth of Shadows.

The First Corridor: The Shadows Awaken

THE MOMENT ELARA STEPPED into the labyrinth, the world around her seemed to shift and change. The light from the entrance faded, leaving her in near-total darkness. The walls of the corridor were smooth and cold, their surfaces slick with moisture. The air was thick and heavy, filled with the scent of damp earth and decay.

Elara's heart raced as she moved cautiously down the corridor, her hand brushing against the wall to guide her steps. The silence was oppressive, broken only by the sound of her own breathing and the faint drip of water echoing through the passageways.

But as she ventured deeper into the labyrinth, the silence was shattered by a low, whispering voice. The sound seemed to come from all around her, echoing off the walls and filling the air with a sense of dread.

"Elara..." the voice whispered, its tone soft and insidious. "You are not strong enough... You are not worthy... Turn back now, before it is too late..."

Elara froze, her breath catching in her throat. The voice was not her own, but it seemed to know her—know her fears, her doubts, her deepest insecurities. It was a voice that spoke to the darkness within her, the part of her that questioned whether she was truly capable of fulfilling the prophecy.

But Elara refused to be swayed by the voice's whispers. She had faced challenges before, had confronted her fears and doubts, and she would not let them defeat her now. With a deep breath, she steadied herself and continued down the corridor, her resolve firm.

The voice continued to whisper, its tone growing more urgent and menacing. "You will fail... You are not strong enough... The darkness will consume you..."

Elara clenched her fists, her heart pounding with a mixture of fear and anger. She knew that the labyrinth was playing tricks on her, trying to undermine her confidence and weaken her resolve. But she would not give in. She had come too far to turn back now.

As she moved deeper into the labyrinth, the whispers grew louder, the voices multiplying until they filled the air with a cacophony of fear and doubt. The walls of the corridor seemed to close in around her, the shadows growing darker and more oppressive.

But Elara pressed on, her mind focused on her goal. She had to find the center of the labyrinth, the heart of the darkness that lay within. Only by confronting the darkness head-on could she hope to overcome it.

Finally, after what felt like hours of walking, Elara reached the end of the corridor. The passageway opened up into a large, circular chamber, its walls lined with mirrors that reflected the dim light of the corridor.

The chamber was eerily silent, the air thick with an overwhelming sense of dread. Elara could see her reflection in the mirrors, but something was wrong—her reflection was distorted, twisted, as if the mirrors were warping her image into something monstrous.

As she stepped into the chamber, the whispers in her mind grew louder, more insistent. The reflections in the mirrors seemed to come to life, their distorted faces sneering and mocking her.

"Look at you," one of the reflections said, its voice filled with venom. "You think you can succeed? You are weak, a failure. You will never fulfill the prophecy."

Elara's heart pounded with fear as she stared at the twisted reflections. The words cut deep, striking at the core of her insecurities. But she knew that she couldn't let the illusions control her. The labyrinth was trying to break her, to make her question her own worth and strength.

"You are nothing," another reflection hissed. "You will never be worthy. The darkness will consume you."

Elara clenched her fists, her breath coming in short, sharp gasps. She could feel the weight of the darkness pressing down on her, trying to suffocate her spirit. But she refused to give in. She had faced her fears before, and she would face them again.

With a deep breath, Elara closed her eyes, shutting out the twisted reflections and the insidious whispers. She focused on the blessings she had received from the gods—wisdom, strength, and compassion. She let those blessings fill her heart and mind, pushing back against the darkness that threatened to overwhelm her.

The whispers in her mind began to fade, their voices growing fainter as Elara's resolve grew stronger. The distorted reflections in the mirrors flickered and wavered, their sneering faces dissolving into shadows.

"You cannot defeat me," Elara whispered, her voice filled with determination. "I am stronger than you. I will not be consumed by the darkness."

The chamber trembled as if in response to her words, the walls of the labyrinth shaking with a low, rumbling sound. The mirrors shattered, their broken pieces scattering across the floor like shards of glass.

The darkness that had filled the chamber began to lift, the oppressive weight of fear and doubt dissipating like mist in the morning sun. Elara opened her eyes, her heart filled with a sense of triumph and relief.

She had passed the first trial of the labyrinth, had confronted her own fears and insecurities, and had emerged stronger and more determined.

But she knew that the journey was far from over. The Labyrinth of Shadows was a place of illusion and deception, and there were still many challenges ahead.

With a deep breath, Elara stepped out of the chamber and continued down the next corridor, her mind focused on the path ahead.

The Twisting Corridors: A Maze of Fear

THE LABYRINTH WAS A maze of twisting, turning corridors, each one more disorienting and treacherous than the last. The walls were smooth and featureless, their surfaces cold to the touch. The air was thick with the scent of damp earth and decay, and the only light came from faint, flickering torches that lined the walls at irregular intervals.

As Elara moved deeper into the labyrinth, the corridors seemed to close in around her, the walls narrowing until they were barely wide enough for her to pass through. The air grew colder, and the darkness pressed in on her like a living thing, its tendrils reaching out to ensnare her.

The whispers in her mind returned, their voices more insidious and menacing than before. They spoke of her deepest fears and doubts, of the darkness that lay within her own soul.

"You cannot escape the darkness," the whispers said, their tone filled with malice. "It is a part of you, a part of who you are. You will never be free of it."

Elara's heart pounded with fear as she listened to the whispers. She could feel the darkness pressing down on her, trying to suffocate her spirit. But she knew that she couldn't let the illusions control her. The labyrinth was trying to break her, to make her question her own worth and strength.

As she turned a corner, Elara came face to face with a wall of shadows, its surface shifting and writhing like a living thing. The shadows reached out to her, their tendrils curling around her arms and legs, pulling her into the darkness.

Elara struggled against the shadows, her heart pounding with fear and desperation. She could feel the darkness closing in on her, its cold, clammy tendrils wrapping around her body like a suffocating shroud.

But even as the shadows pulled her deeper into the darkness, Elara refused to give in. She focused on the blessings she had received from the gods, drawing on the strength and resolve that had carried her through the previous trials.

With a burst of energy, Elara broke free from the shadows, their tendrils dissolving into mist as she pulled herself out of their grasp. The darkness around her lifted, the walls of the labyrinth returning to their cold, featureless state.

Elara took a deep breath, her heart still racing from the encounter. She knew that the labyrinth was testing her, trying to wear down her resolve and break her spirit. But she would not let it succeed. She had faced her fears before, and she would face them again.

As she continued through the labyrinth, Elara encountered more illusions and traps, each one more devious and terrifying than the last. She faced walls that closed in on her, floors that gave way beneath her feet, and shadows that whispered lies and half-truths in her ear.

But with each challenge, Elara grew stronger and more determined. She learned to trust in her own strength and resolve, to push back against the darkness that sought to consume her.

Finally, after what felt like hours of wandering through the twisting corridors, Elara reached a large, open chamber at the center of the labyrinth. The walls of the chamber were lined with dark, swirling shadows, their tendrils reaching out to ensnare her.

But Elara was not afraid. She had faced the darkness before, and she had emerged stronger and more determined. She knew that this was the final challenge of the labyrinth—the heart of the darkness that lay within her own soul.

With a deep breath, Elara stepped into the chamber, her heart filled with resolve and determination. The shadows around her seemed to pulse with energy, their tendrils reaching out to pull her into the darkness.

But Elara stood her ground, her mind focused on the blessings she had received from the gods. She let the strength of those blessings fill her heart and mind, pushing back against the darkness that threatened to overwhelm her.

"You cannot defeat me," Elara whispered, her voice filled with determination. "I am stronger than you. I will not be consumed by the darkness."

The chamber trembled as if in response to her words, the walls of the labyrinth shaking with a low, rumbling sound. The shadows around her flickered and wavered, their tendrils retreating as Elara's resolve grew stronger.

Finally, with a final burst of energy, Elara pushed back against the darkness, the shadows dissolving into mist as the chamber filled with a bright, golden light.

Elara felt a deep sense of triumph and relief as she realized that she had passed the final challenge of the labyrinth. She had confronted her own fears and insecurities, and had emerged stronger and more determined.

With a deep breath, Elara stepped out of the chamber and made her way to the exit of the labyrinth, her heart filled with determination as she prepared to face the final leg of her journey.

The labyrinth had tested her in ways she had never imagined, but she had emerged victorious. She had confronted the darkness within herself, and had proven that she was strong enough to overcome it.

As she stepped out of the labyrinth and into the light of the outside world, Elara knew that she was ready to fulfill her destiny. The journey had been long and arduous, but she was stronger and more determined than ever.

With the blessings of the gods guiding her, Elara set out on the final leg of her journey, her heart filled with hope and resolve. The secrets of the forgotten city awaited, and she was ready to uncover them.

Chapter 9: The Chamber of Memories

The Entrance to the Chamber

The Labyrinth of Shadows had tested Elara's resolve and inner strength, pushing her to confront her deepest fears and emerge stronger. But as she stepped out of the dark corridors and into the heart of the labyrinth, she felt a sense of both relief and trepidation. The challenges she had faced were daunting, but the journey was far from over. Before her lay the Chamber of Memories, the final trial she must undergo before uncovering the forgotten city's secrets.

The Chamber of Memories was not like the other chambers she had encountered. It was a vast, circular room with a high, domed ceiling. The walls were made of polished stone, their surfaces smooth and cold to the touch. The floor was a mosaic of intricate patterns, each tile depicting scenes from the city's past—images of people, places, and events long lost to time.

At the center of the chamber stood a large, ornate pedestal, its surface covered in glowing symbols and runes. The air in the chamber was thick with a sense of history, as if the very walls were alive with the memories of the people who had once lived in the city. Elara could feel their presence, their collective consciousness pressing down on her, filling the air with a palpable energy.

This was the Chamber of Memories, a place where the past was preserved and the secrets of the forgotten city were stored. It was said that those who entered the chamber would experience the city's history firsthand, seeing its triumphs and tragedies through the eyes of its people. But the chamber was also a place of reflection, where one could learn from the mistakes of the past and gain insight into the future.

Elara took a deep breath, her heart pounding with anticipation and apprehension. She knew that the Chamber of Memories held the key to understanding the city's fate, but she also knew that the journey would not be easy. The memories stored within the chamber would be overwhelming, and she would need to keep her wits about her if she hoped to make sense of them.

With a sense of determination, Elara stepped forward and approached the pedestal at the center of the chamber. The symbols on its surface glowed brighter as she drew near, their light casting eerie shadows on the walls.

Elara hesitated for a moment, her hand hovering over the pedestal. She could feel the energy emanating from it, a pulsing rhythm that seemed to resonate with her very soul. The memories of the lost civilization were waiting for her, ready to reveal their secrets.

With a deep breath, Elara placed her hand on the pedestal.

The First Vision: The City of Light

THE MOMENT ELARA'S hand touched the pedestal, the world around her shifted. The polished stone walls of the chamber dissolved, replaced by a dazzling landscape bathed in golden light. The air was warm and fragrant, filled with the scent of blooming flowers and fresh earth. Elara found herself standing on a wide, cobblestone street, lined with trees and bustling with activity.

This was the forgotten city, but not as she had seen it before. This was the city at the height of its power and glory, a place of wonder and beauty that seemed almost too perfect to be real.

Elara looked around in awe, her eyes wide with amazement. The buildings that lined the street were tall and majestic, their facades adorned with intricate carvings and colorful murals. The streets were filled with people, their faces radiant with happiness and contentment as they went about their daily lives.

As Elara walked down the street, she noticed that the people were dressed in fine garments made of shimmering fabrics that seemed to catch the light in a thousand different hues. They moved with a grace and elegance that spoke of a deep sense of purpose and fulfillment.

The city was alive with energy, its streets filled with the sounds of laughter, music, and conversation. Merchants called out to passersby from their stalls, selling everything from fresh produce to finely crafted jewelry. Children ran and played in the streets, their laughter ringing out like music.

Elara felt a sense of wonder as she took in the vibrant scene before her. This was a city that had once been a beacon of hope and progress, a place where people had lived in harmony and prosperity. The air was filled with a sense of possibility, as if anything was possible in this city of light.

As Elara continued to explore the city, she began to notice its technological marvels—wonders that seemed almost magical in their sophistication. Tall, graceful towers rose into the sky, their surfaces covered in gleaming solar panels that absorbed the sunlight and provided power to the entire city. Floating platforms moved effortlessly through the air, carrying people and goods from one part of the city to another.

The streets were lined with devices that emitted a soft, soothing light, illuminating the city in a warm, golden glow. These lights were powered by an advanced energy source that was both clean and sustainable, a testament to the city's commitment to harmony with nature.

Elara marveled at the city's achievements, her heart filled with admiration for the people who had built such a remarkable place. This was a city that had harnessed the power of technology to create a utopia, a place where the challenges of the past had been overcome and where the future seemed bright and full of promise.

But even as Elara marveled at the city's wonders, she couldn't shake the feeling that something was wrong. There was an undercurrent of tension in the air, a sense of unease that seemed to lurk just beneath the surface.

As she continued to explore the city, Elara began to notice the subtle signs of this unease. The people she passed on the street wore smiles, but there was a shadow behind their eyes, a hint of worry and fear that belied their outward happiness. Conversations were filled with talk of progress and prosperity, but there was an undercurrent of doubt and uncertainty.

Elara felt a growing sense of foreboding as she made her way to the city's central square, a large open space surrounded by grand buildings and dominated by a towering statue of a figure holding a glowing orb. The square was filled with people, their faces turned toward a raised platform where a group of leaders stood, their expressions serious and grave.

This was the heart of the city, the place where decisions were made and where the fate of the people was determined. Elara could sense the tension in the air, the weight of the choices that lay before these leaders.

As she watched, one of the leaders stepped forward and began to speak, his voice calm and measured, but filled with a sense of urgency.

"My fellow citizens," the leader said, his voice carrying across the square, "we stand at a crossroads. Our city has achieved greatness, but with that greatness comes responsibility. We have harnessed the power of technology to create a world of abundance and prosperity, but we must not forget the lessons of the past. We must not allow our ambition to blind us to the dangers that lie ahead."

The crowd murmured in agreement, but there was also a note of fear in their voices. Elara could see the worry etched on their faces, the uncertainty that had begun to take root in their hearts.

The leader continued, his voice growing more intense. "We have the power to shape our future, but we must be careful. We must ensure that our actions are guided by wisdom, compassion, and humility. We cannot afford to be reckless, for the consequences could be dire."

Elara felt a chill run down her spine as she listened to the leader's words. The city's achievements were undeniable, but they had come at a cost. The people were beginning to realize that their pursuit of progress and prosperity had brought them to the edge of a precipice, and that one wrong step could lead to disaster.

The vision began to blur and fade, the bright, golden light of the city dimming as the world around Elara shifted once again.

The Second Vision: The Fall of the City

THE LIGHT FADED COMPLETELY, and Elara found herself standing in the same central square, but the scene before her was drastically different. The once-vibrant city was now a place of ruin and despair. The buildings that had once stood tall and proud were now crumbling, their facades cracked and broken. The streets, once filled with laughter and music, were now eerily silent, their cobblestones slick with rain and littered with debris.

The air was thick with the scent of smoke and ash, and the sky above was dark and stormy, filled with swirling clouds that seemed to press down on the city like a heavy shroud. The people who had once walked these streets with grace and purpose were now huddled in small groups, their faces gaunt and hollow, their eyes filled with despair.

Elara's heart ached as she took in the devastation around her. This was the same city she had just seen in all its glory, but now it was a place of ruin, its people broken and defeated.

As she walked through the streets, Elara noticed that the technological marvels that had once powered the city were now silent and lifeless. The solar panels on the towers were cracked and shattered, their surfaces covered in a thick layer of soot. The floating platforms that had once moved effortlessly through the air were now grounded, their mechanisms frozen and rusted.

The city that had once been a beacon of hope and progress was now a graveyard, its achievements reduced to nothing more than a distant memory.

Elara continued to walk through the desolate streets, her heart heavy with sorrow. She could feel the weight of the city's fall pressing down on her, the sense of loss and regret that seemed to hang in the air like a pall.

As she approached the central square, Elara saw a group of people gathered around a large, cracked statue—the same statue that had once stood proudly in the square, its glowing orb a symbol of the city's power and potential. But now the orb was dark, its light extinguished, and the statue itself was broken, its features worn away by time and neglect.

The people gathered around the statue were silent, their faces filled with a mixture of anger and despair. Elara could sense their pain, the bitterness that had taken root in their hearts as they realized the extent of their loss.

As she watched, one of the people stepped forward, a woman with long, tangled hair and eyes that burned with a fierce, desperate intensity. She raised her hands toward the statue, her voice filled with anger and frustration.

"We were promised a better future," the woman cried, her voice echoing through the square. "We were told that our city would be a beacon of hope, a place where we could build a better world for ourselves and our children. But what have we gained? What have we achieved? Nothing but ruin and despair!"

The crowd murmured in agreement, their voices filled with anger and bitterness. Elara could feel the weight of their emotions pressing down on her, the sense of betrayal that had taken hold of their hearts.

The woman continued, her voice growing more intense. "We were blinded by our own ambition, by our desire for power and progress. We thought we could control the forces of nature, that we could bend the will of the gods to our own desires. But we were wrong. We were foolish and arrogant, and now we are paying the price for our hubris."

Elara's heart ached as she listened to the woman's words. The city's fall had not been the result of some external force, but of its own people's actions. They had pushed too far, reached too high, and in doing so, they had brought about their own destruction.

The vision began to shift, the scene blurring and fading as the world around Elara changed once again.

The Third Vision: The Final Moments

THE DARKNESS LIFTED, and Elara found herself standing in a grand hall, its walls lined with shelves filled with ancient scrolls and tomes. The air was thick with the scent of old parchment and ink, and the only light came from a series of flickering candles that cast long, dancing shadows on the walls.

This was the city's great library, the repository of its knowledge and wisdom. But now it was a place of desperation, a place where the city's leaders had gathered in a last-ditch effort to save what remained of their civilization.

Elara could see the leaders standing around a large, ornate table, their faces etched with worry and fear. They were the same leaders she had seen in the earlier vision, but now they were older, their faces lined with the weight of their decisions.

The leader who had spoken in the square was there, his once-strong voice now filled with a note of desperation as he addressed the others.

"We have no choice," the leader said, his voice trembling. "The city is falling apart. The power we unleashed is beyond our control. If we do not act now, everything will be lost."

The others murmured in agreement, their voices filled with despair. Elara could see the fear in their eyes, the realization that they were facing the end of their civilization.

One of the leaders, a woman with silver hair and sharp, piercing eyes, stepped forward and placed a large, glowing crystal on the table. The crystal pulsed with a faint, rhythmic light, casting an eerie glow over the room.

"This is our last hope," the woman said, her voice filled with a sense of urgency. "The crystal contains the knowledge and power of our people, the culmination of all our achievements. If we can harness its energy, we may be able to stabilize the city, to prevent its complete collapse."

The others nodded, their faces filled with a mixture of hope and fear. Elara could see that they were desperate, willing to try anything to save their city.

But even as the leaders prepared to activate the crystal, Elara could sense that something was wrong. The air in the room was thick with tension, the very walls seeming to pulse with an unseen energy. The crystal's light grew brighter, its glow intensifying until it filled the entire room with a blinding, white light.

And then, without warning, the crystal shattered.

The light exploded outward, filling the room with a deafening roar as the energy it contained was released in a violent, uncontrolled burst. The walls of the library trembled and cracked, the shelves collapsing as the force of the explosion ripped through the room.

Elara felt a wave of heat and pressure wash over her, knocking her to the ground as the room dissolved into chaos. The leaders were thrown back, their bodies crumpling to the floor as the energy of the crystal consumed everything in its path.

The vision began to blur and fade, the world around Elara dissolving into darkness as the final moments of the city played out before her eyes.

The Aftermath: A Lesson Learned

THE DARKNESS LIFTED, and Elara found herself back in the Chamber of Memories, her hand still resting on the pedestal at the center of the room. The visions had ended, but the weight of what she had seen remained with her, a heavy burden that pressed down on her heart.

The city had been a place of wonder and beauty, a beacon of hope and progress that had achieved greatness beyond imagination. But it had also been a place of hubris and arrogance, where the people had pushed too far, reached too high, and in doing so, had brought about their own destruction.

Elara felt a deep sense of sorrow as she realized the full extent of the city's fall. The people had been blinded by their own ambition, their desire for power and progress leading them to forget the lessons of the past. They had believed that they could control the forces of nature, that they could bend the will of the gods to their own desires. But in the end, they had paid the price for their hubris.

But even as Elara mourned the loss of the city, she knew that there was a lesson to be learned from its fall. The memories stored within the Chamber of Memories were not just a record of the past—they were a warning, a reminder of the dangers of unchecked ambition and the importance of wisdom, compassion, and humility.

The city's achievements had been remarkable, but they had come at a cost. The people had lost sight of what truly mattered, and in doing so, they had brought about their own downfall.

Elara knew that she had to carry the lessons of the city with her, to ensure that the mistakes of the past were not repeated. The blessings of the gods—wisdom, strength, and compassion—had guided her through the trials of the labyrinth, and now they would guide her as she sought to uncover the secrets of the forgotten city and fulfill her destiny.

With a deep breath, Elara removed her hand from the pedestal and stepped back from the Chamber of Memories. The visions had ended, but the weight of what she had seen remained with her, a heavy burden that she would carry with her on the final leg of her journey.

The journey had been long and arduous, filled with challenges and trials that had tested her in ways she had never imagined. But Elara knew that she was stronger and more determined than ever. The lessons of the past had been revealed to her, and she was ready to use that knowledge to shape the future.

With the blessings of the gods guiding her, Elara stepped out of the Chamber of Memories and made her way to the exit of the labyrinth. The secrets of the forgotten city awaited, and she was ready to uncover them. The journey was far from over, but Elara knew that she was ready to face whatever challenges lay ahead.

The lessons of the past had been learned, and the future was hers to shape.

Chapter 10: The City of Echoes

Arrival at the Forgotten City

The journey had been long and arduous, fraught with trials that tested every facet of Elara's being. But as she emerged from the labyrinth and took her first steps toward the forgotten city, she felt a mix of awe and trepidation. The city lay before her, a once-glorious metropolis now shrouded in an eerie silence that seemed to stretch out infinitely, as if time itself had forgotten this place.

The landscape surrounding the city was a mixture of stark beauty and haunting decay. Towering mountains framed the skyline, their peaks piercing the sky like ancient sentinels. The air was thick with the scent of damp earth and moss, a testament to nature's relentless reclaiming of what once belonged to man. The forgotten city was a place caught between two worlds—the world of the past, where it had thrived as a beacon of progress and enlightenment, and the world of the present, where it stood as a monument to hubris and the inexorable march of time.

Elara's heart pounded as she took in the sight of the city's towering structures, their facades cracked and weathered but still standing with a dignity that defied the centuries. The architecture was unlike anything she had ever seen—grand, imposing, and intricate, with arches that soared into the heavens and spires that reached for the sky. Yet, despite the city's majesty, there was a melancholy air about it, as if the stones themselves were mourning the loss of the people who had once called this place home.

The silence was profound, broken only by the occasional rustle of leaves and the distant call of a bird. There was no sign of life in the city, no movement in the streets, no voices to be heard. It was as if the entire metropolis had been frozen in time, preserved in a state of perpetual twilight. The buildings stood like ancient monoliths, their windows dark and empty, their doorways sealed by the creeping vines and overgrowth that had claimed them.

Elara took a deep breath, steeling herself for what lay ahead. The forgotten city held the answers she sought, the key to understanding its tragic fate and uncovering the secrets that had been buried for so long. But she knew that the journey through the city would not be easy. The echoes of the past lingered here, waiting to be awakened, and she would need to navigate their memories carefully if she hoped to uncover the truth.

With a sense of purpose, Elara stepped forward, her feet crunching on the gravel of the overgrown path as she made her way toward the city's gates. The path was lined with statues of long-forgotten gods and heroes, their features worn smooth by the passage of time but still exuding an aura of power and majesty. Each statue seemed to watch her as she passed, their eyes filled with a silent, eternal vigilance.

The gates of the city loomed ahead, massive and imposing, their iron bars twisted and rusted with age. The gates had once been a symbol of the city's strength and security, but now they stood as a barrier between the present and the past, guarding the secrets that lay within.

Elara hesitated for a moment, her hand resting on the cold, rough surface of the gate. She could feel the weight of the city's history pressing down on her, the echoes of its former inhabitants whispering just beyond the threshold. With a deep breath, she pushed the gates open, the creaking of the iron echoing through the silent streets.

As the gates swung open, Elara stepped into the forgotten city, her heart filled with a mixture of awe and reverence. The journey had begun.

The Silent Streets

THE STREETS OF THE forgotten city were wide and expansive, their surfaces covered in a thin layer of dust and debris. The once-gleaming cobblestones were cracked and uneven, the mortar between them crumbling away with the passage of time. Nature had begun to reclaim the city, with vines and ivy creeping up the walls of buildings, their roots burrowing into the cracks and crevices, slowly pulling the structures back into the earth.

Elara walked slowly, her footsteps echoing in the silence, the only sound in a city that had once been filled with the hustle and bustle of daily life. The air was heavy with the scent of decay, mixed with the earthy aroma of damp moss and lichen. It was as if the city itself was breathing, its slow, steady exhalations filling the air with a sense of melancholy.

As Elara moved deeper into the city, she began to notice the details of its architecture—the intricate carvings that adorned the facades of buildings, the delicate filigree that framed windows and doorways, the towering columns that supported grand archways. Each building was a masterpiece of craftsmanship, a testament to the skill and creativity of the people who had once lived here.

But despite the beauty of the city, there was a sense of unease that lingered in the air, a feeling that something was not quite right. The city was too quiet, too still, as if it was waiting for something—or someone—to awaken it from its long slumber.

Elara's heart raced as she made her way toward the city's central square, the focal point of the metropolis where the grandest structures stood. The square was vast and open, its cobblestones arranged in intricate patterns that formed a giant mosaic depicting scenes from the city's history. The images were faded and worn, their colors muted by time, but they still conveyed a sense of grandeur and importance.

At the center of the square stood a massive fountain, its basin filled with stagnant water that reflected the overcast sky above. The fountain was adorned with statues of gods and goddesses, their forms frozen in graceful poses, their faces serene and composed. Water no longer flowed from the fountain's spouts, but the intricate carvings of waves and ripples on its surface hinted at the life and energy that had once filled this place.

Elara approached the fountain, her eyes drawn to the statues that surrounded it. Each figure was depicted with a level of detail that was almost lifelike, their expressions filled with a sense of calm and peace. But as she looked closer, Elara noticed something strange—each statue's eyes were closed, as if they were in a deep, eternal sleep.

The silence in the square was oppressive, the air heavy with a sense of anticipation. Elara could feel the weight of the city's history pressing down on her, the echoes of its former inhabitants whispering just beyond her reach. She knew that the city was trying to tell her something, but she couldn't quite grasp what it was.

As she stood by the fountain, Elara closed her eyes and focused on the sounds around her. The silence was almost deafening, but beneath it, she could hear faint whispers, like the rustling of leaves in the wind. The whispers were soft and indistinct, but they seemed to be coming from the very walls of the city, as if the stones themselves were trying to speak to her.

Elara listened carefully, her heart pounding in her chest as she tried to make out the words. The whispers grew louder, more insistent, until they filled her mind with a cacophony of voices, each one speaking in a language she couldn't understand.

But as the whispers reached a crescendo, Elara felt a sudden jolt, as if something deep within her had been awakened. The whispers fell silent, and in their place, she heard a single, clear voice—a voice filled with sorrow and regret.

"Welcome, Elara," the voice said, its tone gentle and mournful. "You have come far, and now you stand at the heart of the city. But the journey is not yet over. The echoes of the past are waiting to be heard, and it is through them that you will learn the truth of what happened here."

Elara's eyes snapped open, her breath coming in short, sharp gasps. The voice had been so clear, so real, as if it had been spoken directly into her mind. She looked around the square, but there was no one there—only the statues and the empty streets.

The city was alive, but not in the way she had expected. It was alive with memories, with the echoes of the people who had once lived here. And it was through these echoes that she would learn the truth.

With a sense of purpose, Elara stepped away from the fountain and began to explore the city's streets, guided by the echoes of the past.

The Echoes of the Past

AS ELARA WALKED THROUGH the city, the echoes grew stronger, their voices filling her mind with a torrent of memories and emotions. The city was a vast repository of the collective experiences of its inhabitants, each building, each street, each stone holding a fragment of the past. The echoes were not just voices—they were memories, impressions left behind by the people who had once called this place home.

Elara felt as if she was walking through a dream, the boundaries between reality and memory blurring as the echoes guided her through the city. She saw the city as it had once been, vibrant and full of life, its streets bustling with people and activity. The buildings were pristine, their facades gleaming in the sunlight, their windows filled with the light of a thousand candles.

The echoes showed her the daily lives of the city's inhabitants—their joys and sorrows, their hopes and fears, their triumphs and failures. She saw families gathered around dinner tables, sharing meals and stories; children playing in the streets, their laughter ringing out like music; artisans at work, their hands crafting beautiful works of art and architecture.

But as Elara delved deeper into the city's memories, the echoes began to show her darker, more troubling scenes. She saw the city's leaders in their grand halls, debating the future of their civilization, their faces etched with worry and doubt. She saw scientists and engineers working in secret laboratories, their hands trembling as they manipulated strange and powerful energies.

The city had been a place of progress and innovation, but it had also been a place of ambition and hubris. The people had reached for the stars, believing that they could conquer any challenge, overcome any obstacle. But in their quest for greatness, they had unleashed forces they could not control—forces that had ultimately led to their downfall.

Elara's heart ached as she witnessed the city's final moments, the echoes showing her the destruction that had befallen the once-great metropolis. The sky had darkened, the air filled with the scent of burning wood and melting stone. The city had been consumed by chaos, its streets filled with the sounds of screaming and weeping as the buildings crumbled and the ground shook beneath the people's feet.

The echoes showed her the desperate attempts of the city's leaders to save what remained of their civilization, their voices filled with a mixture of hope and despair as they activated the crystal that contained the knowledge and power of their people. But the crystal's energy had been too much, too unstable, and it had shattered, unleashing a wave of destruction that had swept through the city, leaving nothing but ruin in its wake.

Elara felt tears streaming down her face as she experienced the city's fall through the eyes of its inhabitants. The echoes of their pain and regret were almost too much to bear, but she knew that she had to see this through to the end. The city's fate had been sealed by the choices of its people, and she needed to understand those choices if she was to prevent history from repeating itself.

As the final echoes of the city's destruction faded away, Elara found herself standing in front of a large, ornate building that had once been the city's central library. The building was one of the few structures that had remained relatively intact, its grand facade still standing despite the passage of time.

Elara felt a sense of anticipation as she approached the library's entrance. The echoes had guided her here, to this place, and she knew that the answers she sought lay within.

With a deep breath, she pushed open the heavy wooden doors and stepped inside.

The Library of Echoes

THE INTERIOR OF THE library was vast and cavernous, its walls lined with towering shelves filled with ancient scrolls and tomes. The air was thick with the scent of old parchment and ink, and the only light came from a series of flickering candles that cast long, dancing shadows on the walls.

The library was a place of knowledge and learning, a repository of the city's collective wisdom. But it was also a place of memories, a place where the echoes of the past were preserved and guarded. Elara could feel their presence as she walked through the aisles, the whispers of the city's inhabitants filling the air like a soft, mournful chant.

As she explored the library, Elara's eyes were drawn to a large, circular table in the center of the room. The table was covered in a thick layer of dust, but beneath it, she could see the faint outlines of strange symbols and runes, their surfaces glowing with a faint, otherworldly light.

Elara felt a sense of déjà vu as she approached the table, her heart pounding in her chest. She had seen this table before, in the visions the echoes had shown her. It was here that the city's leaders had made their final, desperate attempt to save their civilization. It was here that the crystal had shattered, unleashing the wave of destruction that had consumed the city.

The echoes grew stronger as Elara placed her hand on the table, their voices filling her mind with a torrent of memories and emotions. She could feel the weight of the city's history pressing down on her, the collective experiences of its people overwhelming her senses.

But amidst the chaos of the echoes, Elara sensed something else—something deeper, more ancient. It was a presence, a consciousness that had been buried beneath the layers of memory and time. It was the voice of the city itself, the voice of the forgotten metropolis that had once been a beacon of hope and progress.

"Elara," the voice said, its tone gentle and sorrowful. "You have come far, and now you stand at the heart of the city. But there is still much you do not know. The answers you seek are not just in the past—they are within you. The choices you make will determine the future of this world."

Elara felt a shiver run down her spine as the voice spoke to her. It was as if the city itself was reaching out to her, guiding her toward the truth.

"The city fell because of the choices of its people," the voice continued. "They sought power and progress, but they lost sight of what truly mattered. They forgot the importance of wisdom, compassion, and humility. They believed they could control the forces of nature, that they could bend the will of the gods to their own desires. But they were wrong."

Elara's heart ached as she listened to the voice. The city's fall had not been the result of some external force, but of the choices its people had made. They had been blinded by their own ambition, and in their pursuit of greatness, they had brought about their own destruction.

"But there is still hope," the voice said, its tone filled with a sense of urgency. "You have the power to change the future, to ensure that the mistakes of the past are not repeated. The knowledge and power of the city are within your reach, but you must use them wisely. You must remember the lessons of the past and carry them with you as you move forward."

Elara felt a surge of determination as the voice spoke to her. The journey had been long and difficult, but she knew that she was ready to face whatever challenges lay ahead. The city had given her the answers she sought, and now it was up to her to use that knowledge to shape the future.

With a deep breath, Elara removed her hand from the table and stepped back from the library. The echoes of the past had revealed their secrets, and now it was time for her to take the next step on her journey.

The city had fallen, but its legacy would live on. And Elara would ensure that the lessons of the past were not forgotten.

The Echoes Fade

AS ELARA LEFT THE LIBRARY and stepped back into the streets of the forgotten city, she felt a sense of closure and resolve. The echoes of the past had guided her through the city, revealing the secrets that had been buried for so long. But now, as she walked through the silent streets, the echoes began to fade, their voices growing fainter until they were nothing more than distant memories.

The city was still and silent, but it no longer felt oppressive or foreboding. There was a sense of peace in the air, as if the city had finally come to terms with its past and was ready to move forward.

Elara walked slowly, her eyes taking in the details of the city's architecture, the intricate carvings and delicate filigree that adorned its buildings. The city was a place of beauty and wonder, but it was also a place of tragedy, a reminder of the dangers of unchecked ambition and the importance of wisdom, compassion, and humility.

As she made her way to the city's gates, Elara felt a sense of anticipation and excitement. The journey was far from over, but she knew that she was ready to face whatever challenges lay ahead. The city had given her the answers she sought, and now it was up to her to use that knowledge to shape the future.

With a deep breath, Elara stepped out of the forgotten city and into the light of the outside world. The echoes of the past had faded, but their lessons would remain with her always.

The journey had begun, and Elara was ready to fulfill her destiny.

Chapter 11: The Curse of the Lost Civilization

The Heart of the City

The forgotten city had revealed its secrets to Elara in ways she had never imagined. As she stood outside the grand central tower, the last remaining structure of its kind in the metropolis, she felt the weight of the knowledge she had gained pressing down on her like a leaden cloak. The echoes of the past had shown her the rise and fall of this once-great civilization, a place of beauty and innovation that had ultimately been brought to ruin by its own hubris. But there was one final mystery that remained—a dark secret that lay at the heart of the city's downfall.

The central tower loomed above her, its spire piercing the sky like a dagger aimed at the heavens. The tower had once been the pride of the city, a symbol of its power and ambition. It was here that the city's leaders had conducted their most ambitious experiments, harnessing energies and forces that had long been hidden from mortal understanding. But it was also here, deep within the bowels of the tower, that the curse that had destroyed the city had been born.

The curse had not been a simple spell or a hex cast by some vengeful sorcerer. It was something far more insidious, something that had been created by the city's own hands—a powerful artifact known as the Heart of the City. This artifact, a relic of immense power and dark magic, had been the source of the city's greatness, but it had also been its undoing. The Heart had granted the city's leaders the ability to bend reality to their will, to reshape the world according to their desires. But in their pursuit of power, they had unleashed forces they could not control, and the Heart had turned against them, cursing the city and preventing its resurgence.

Elara knew that if she was to fulfill her destiny and bring peace to the city's restless spirits, she would have to find the Heart of the City and break the curse that had doomed the civilization. The path before her was fraught with danger, but she had come too far to turn back now. The echoes of the past had guided her to this point, and she was ready to face whatever challenges lay ahead.

With a sense of determination, Elara stepped forward and entered the central tower.

The Descent into Darkness

THE INTERIOR OF THE tower was a stark contrast to the grandeur of its exterior. The walls were made of cold, dark stone, their surfaces rough and uneven. The air was thick with dust and the scent of decay, and the only light came from the faint glow of ancient runes etched into the stone. The runes pulsed with a dim, sickly light, casting eerie shadows on the walls.

Elara's footsteps echoed through the empty halls as she made her way deeper into the tower. The silence was oppressive, broken only by the occasional creak of the stone and the distant drip of water. The deeper she descended, the colder the air became, until it felt as if the very warmth was being sucked out of the atmosphere.

As she descended a winding staircase, Elara began to feel the weight of the dark magic that permeated the tower. It was a heavy, suffocating presence that pressed down on her like a physical force, making it difficult to breathe. The air was thick with the remnants of the curse, the dark energies that had been unleashed by the Heart of the City and had brought about the civilization's downfall.

Elara knew that she was getting closer to the source of the curse, and the thought filled her with a mixture of fear and determination. The Heart of the City was the key to everything, the source of the city's power and its destruction. She had to find it, to understand it, if she was to have any hope of breaking the curse.

Finally, after what felt like hours of descending into the depths of the tower, Elara reached the lowest level—a vast, cavernous chamber that was completely dark except for the faint, pulsating light of the runes on the walls. The chamber was filled with a deep, foreboding silence, broken only by the distant, rhythmic thrum of energy that seemed to emanate from the very walls.

Elara felt a chill run down her spine as she stepped into the chamber, her eyes straining to see in the dim light. The darkness was so thick that it felt almost tangible, as if it was a living, breathing entity that had been waiting for her to arrive.

At the center of the chamber, bathed in the sickly light of the runes, stood a massive, ornate pedestal. The pedestal was covered in intricate carvings, its surface worn smooth by time. And resting atop the pedestal, glowing with an ominous, otherworldly light, was the Heart of the City.

The Heart of the City Revealed

THE HEART OF THE CITY was a large, crystalline artifact, its surface smooth and flawless, but pulsing with a dark, swirling energy that seemed to move within it like a living thing. The crystal was a deep, blood-red color, its facets catching the dim light and refracting it into a thousand different shades of crimson. The energy within the crystal was palpable, a seething, roiling force that seemed barely contained by the artifact's physical form.

Elara felt a wave of nausea as she approached the Heart, the dark energy radiating from it filling the air with a sense of dread and despair. The closer she got, the stronger the feeling became, until it felt as if the very air was vibrating with the force of the magic contained within the crystal.

But despite the overwhelming sense of fear and revulsion that filled her, Elara couldn't help but be fascinated by the Heart. It was a thing of terrible beauty, a creation of immense power and complexity. The city's leaders had created it to be a source of limitless energy, a way to harness the very forces of nature and bend them to their will. But in doing so, they had created something that was far beyond their understanding or control.

As Elara stared into the depths of the crystal, she could see the energies swirling within it, their movements chaotic and unpredictable. The magic within the Heart was ancient and primal, a force that had existed long before the city had been built. It was a power that could not be controlled, only contained—and even that containment was tenuous at best.

The Heart had been the city's greatest achievement, but it had also been its greatest mistake. The leaders had believed that they could use the Heart to create a utopia, a perfect society where all their desires could be fulfilled. But in their arrogance, they had failed to see the dangers of wielding such power, and the Heart had turned on them, unleashing a curse that had destroyed everything they had built.

Elara reached out a trembling hand toward the Heart, her fingers brushing against its smooth, cold surface. The moment her skin made contact with the crystal, she felt a surge of energy rush through her, filling her mind with a torrent of images and emotions.

She saw the city as it had once been, vibrant and full of life, its streets filled with people and activity. She saw the leaders of the city gathered around the Heart, their faces filled with awe and reverence as they activated the crystal and unleashed its power. She saw the moment when everything went wrong, the moment when the Heart's energies spiraled out of control and unleashed the curse that had destroyed the city.

The images were overwhelming, filling her mind with a cacophony of voices and emotions. She could feel the fear and despair of the people as the city crumbled around them, the pain and regret of the leaders as they realized the extent of their mistake. And beneath it all, she could feel the dark, malevolent presence of the curse, a force that had been born from the Heart's energies and had grown stronger with each passing moment.

Elara pulled her hand away from the crystal, gasping for breath as the images and emotions faded from her mind. The curse was not just a result of the Heart's power—it was a living, breathing entity, a dark force that had been created by the city's hubris and had fed on the despair and suffering of its people.

The Heart of the City was the source of the curse, but it was also the key to breaking it. Elara knew that if she could find a way to neutralize the Heart's energies, to contain the dark magic within it, she could lift the curse and bring peace to the city's restless spirits.

But the task before her was daunting. The Heart was a creation of immense power, and the curse that it had unleashed was deeply entrenched in the very fabric of the city. Breaking the curse would require more than just physical strength—it would require wisdom, compassion, and a deep understanding of the forces at play.

Elara knew that she could not do this alone. The blessings of the gods had guided her through the trials of the labyrinth and the city, and now they would guide her as she sought to break the curse and bring peace to the city's people.

With a deep breath, Elara steeled herself for the task ahead and began to search the chamber for anything that could help her neutralize the Heart's dark magic.

The Search for Answers

THE CHAMBER WAS VAST and filled with shadows, the dim light of the runes casting long, flickering shadows on the walls. Elara knew that the answers she sought were hidden somewhere within the chamber, buried beneath the layers of time and memory.

As she explored the chamber, Elara's eyes were drawn to a series of ancient tomes and scrolls that were scattered across a nearby table. The table was covered in dust, but the runes on the covers of the books still glowed faintly, their surfaces etched with symbols that seemed to pulse with a life of their own.

Elara carefully picked up one of the tomes, brushing away the dust to reveal the title etched into the cover: **The Heart of the City: A Treatise on Power and Destruction.** The title sent a shiver down her spine, but she knew that this was exactly what she had been looking for.

She opened the tome, the pages yellowed and brittle with age, and began to read. The text was dense and filled with arcane language, but Elara's keen mind quickly deciphered its meaning. The tome detailed the creation of the Heart, the experiments that had been conducted to harness its power, and the eventual realization that the Heart was far more dangerous than anyone had anticipated.

The tome spoke of the dark magic that had been infused into the Heart, a magic that had been drawn from the very forces of nature and twisted by the ambitions of the city's leaders. The Heart had been created to be a source of limitless energy, but in doing so, they had inadvertently created a vessel for dark and malevolent forces.

The curse that had destroyed the city was not just a side effect of the Heart's power—it was an intentional act of retribution by the dark forces that had been imprisoned within the crystal. The leaders had believed that they could control these forces, but they had been wrong, and the curse had been their punishment.

Elara's heart sank as she realized the full extent of the challenge before her. The Heart was a creation of immense power, but it was also a creation of immense evil. Neutralizing the Heart's energies would require not just physical strength, but also the ability to confront and overcome the dark forces that had been unleashed by the curse.

But as she continued to read, Elara found a glimmer of hope. The tome spoke of a ritual, a way to neutralize the Heart's dark magic and lift the curse that had been placed on the city. The ritual was complex and dangerous, requiring a deep understanding of the Heart's energies and the ability to channel the blessings of the gods.

The ritual would require Elara to confront the dark forces within the Heart, to face them head-on and use the power of the blessings she had received to neutralize their influence. It would be a battle of wills, a struggle between light and darkness, and the outcome would determine the fate of the city.

Elara felt a surge of determination as she finished reading the tome. The task before her was daunting, but she knew that she was ready to face it. The journey had brought her to this point, and she was prepared to do whatever it took to break the curse and bring peace to the city's people.

With a deep breath, Elara set the tome aside and began to prepare for the ritual.

The Ritual Begins

THE RITUAL WAS A COMPLEX and intricate process, requiring Elara to draw on all of her knowledge and strength. She carefully followed the instructions in the tome, inscribing the runes and symbols on the floor of the chamber, each one glowing with a faint, otherworldly light as she completed it.

The air in the chamber grew heavy with the scent of incense and the faint, metallic tang of magic. The runes on the walls pulsed with energy, their light growing brighter as the ritual progressed. The Heart of the City, still resting on its pedestal, began to hum with a low, resonant tone, its dark energies swirling more violently within the crystal.

Elara could feel the dark forces within the Heart awakening, their presence growing stronger and more malevolent with each passing moment. The curse that had been unleashed on the city was not just a spell—it was a living, breathing entity, a force of darkness that had been feeding on the pain and suffering of the city's people for centuries.

But Elara was not afraid. She had faced darkness before, had confronted her own fears and insecurities in the labyrinth, and had emerged stronger and more determined. The blessings of the gods were with her, and she knew that she could overcome whatever challenges lay ahead.

As she completed the final inscription, Elara stepped back and took a deep breath. The ritual was ready to begin.

She approached the Heart of the City, her hand trembling as she reached out to touch the crystal. The moment her fingers made contact with the smooth surface, she felt a surge of energy rush through her, filling her mind with a torrent of images and emotions.

She saw the city as it had once been, vibrant and full of life, its people filled with hope and ambition. She saw the moment when the Heart had been created, the leaders of the city standing around the crystal, their faces filled with awe and reverence. And she saw the moment when everything had gone wrong, when the dark forces within the Heart had been unleashed and the curse had been born.

The images were overwhelming, filling her mind with a cacophony of voices and emotions. But Elara forced herself to focus, to push through the chaos and find the thread of light that would guide her through the darkness.

She began to chant the words of the ritual, her voice steady and clear despite the turmoil in her mind. The runes on the floor glowed brighter, their light filling the chamber with a soft, golden glow. The dark energies within the Heart began to thrash and writhe, as if they were trying to escape, but Elara held firm, her will unyielding.

As she chanted, she felt the blessings of the gods flowing through her, their power filling her with a sense of peace and strength. The dark forces within the Heart pushed back, their presence growing more intense and malevolent, but Elara refused to give in. She knew that this was the final battle, the ultimate test of her resolve and strength.

The Heart of the City began to pulse with a blinding light, its energies swirling faster and faster as the ritual reached its climax. The dark forces within the crystal screamed and howled, their voices filled with anger and desperation, but Elara's voice rose above them, her chant steady and unwavering.

With a final, powerful surge of energy, Elara completed the ritual, her voice ringing out through the chamber like a clarion call. The runes on the floor and walls glowed with a brilliant, golden light, their energy converging on the Heart of the City.

For a moment, there was silence. The dark energies within the Heart seemed to freeze, their movements suspended in time. And then, with a deafening roar, the crystal shattered, its dark energies exploding outward in a blinding flash of light.

Elara was thrown back, her body slamming into the cold stone floor as the chamber was filled with a torrent of light and sound. The dark forces within the Heart screamed in agony as they were torn apart by the power of the ritual, their presence dissolving into nothingness as the curse was broken.

When the light finally faded, Elara lay on the floor of the chamber, her body trembling with exhaustion. The Heart of the City was gone, its dark magic neutralized and its curse lifted. The chamber was silent, the air filled with a sense of peace and tranquility that had not been felt in centuries.

Elara slowly pushed herself to her feet, her body aching but her heart filled with a sense of triumph. She had done it. She had broken the curse that had destroyed the city and brought peace to its restless spirits.

The Aftermath

AS ELARA MADE HER WAY out of the central tower, the city around her seemed to come alive. The air was filled with a soft, golden light, the runes on the buildings glowing with a gentle, peaceful energy. The oppressive silence that had hung over the city was gone, replaced by the soft rustling of leaves and the distant call of birds.

The city was still a place of ruin and decay, its buildings crumbling and overgrown with vines and ivy. But there was a sense of peace in the air, a feeling that the city was finally at rest.

Elara walked through the streets, her heart filled with a sense of fulfillment. The journey had been long and difficult, but she had achieved what she had set out to do. The city's curse had been broken, and its people could finally find peace.

As she reached the city's gates, Elara turned to take one last look at the forgotten metropolis. The city had been a place of greatness and tragedy, a reminder of the dangers of unchecked ambition and the importance of wisdom, compassion, and humility. But it had also been a place of beauty and wonder, a testament to the creativity and ingenuity of its people.

Elara knew that the lessons she had learned here would stay with her forever. The city had given her the answers she sought, and now it was time for her to take those lessons and use them to shape the future.

With a deep breath, Elara stepped out of the city and into the light of the outside world. The journey was far from over, but she knew that she was ready to face whatever challenges lay ahead.

The curse of the lost civilization had been broken, and the future was hers to shape.

Chapter 12: The Heart of the City

The Confrontation

Elara stood at the entrance of the central tower, her heart pounding in her chest as she stared up at the looming structure. The tower had once been the heart of the city, the place where its greatest minds had gathered to unlock the secrets of the universe. Now, it was a place of shadows and echoes, haunted by the remnants of a civilization that had fallen into ruin.

The journey through the forgotten city had been arduous, filled with trials that had tested Elara's strength, wisdom, and resolve. She had uncovered the city's secrets, learned of its tragic fate, and discovered the source of the curse that had destroyed it. But there was still one final task that remained—the Heart of the City, the artifact that had granted the civilization its immense power, but had also led to its destruction.

Elara knew that the Heart was not just a simple artifact. It was a living, pulsating crystal, filled with dark magic and a will of its own. The curse that had been unleashed upon the city had originated from the Heart, and its power still lingered within the tower, waiting for someone to release it.

The thought filled Elara with a mixture of fear and determination. She knew that the Heart was dangerous, that it had the power to tempt and corrupt even the strongest of wills. But she also knew that she was the only one who could break its hold, the only one who could lift the curse and bring peace to the city's restless spirits.

With a deep breath, Elara steeled herself and stepped into the tower.

The Descent

THE INTERIOR OF THE tower was cold and dark, the air thick with the scent of damp stone and decay. The walls were smooth and featureless, their surfaces worn by the passage of time. The only light came from the faint glow of ancient runes that lined the walls, their dim light casting eerie shadows in the corners of the room.

As Elara descended deeper into the tower, the air grew colder, and the sense of dread that had been building within her intensified. The darkness seemed to press in on her from all sides, as if the very walls were closing in, trapping her within the tower's depths.

The silence was oppressive, broken only by the soft sound of Elara's footsteps echoing off the stone floor. But as she continued to descend, she began to hear another sound—a low, rhythmic thrum that seemed to resonate through the very bones of the tower. It was a sound that filled her with both awe and fear, a sound that seemed to emanate from the very heart of the tower.

Elara knew that she was getting closer to the Heart of the City, the source of the curse and the object of her final trial. The thought filled her with a mixture of anticipation and dread, but she pressed on, determined to see her journey through to the end.

Finally, after what felt like an eternity, Elara reached the bottom of the tower. The air was so cold that it burned her lungs with each breath, and the darkness was so thick that she could barely see a few feet in front of her. But she could feel the presence of the Heart, its power radiating out from the chamber at the end of the corridor.

With a deep breath, Elara summoned the blessings of the gods, feeling their warmth and strength flow through her. The fear that had been gnawing at her heart began to fade, replaced by a sense of resolve and determination.

She took one final step and entered the chamber.

The Heart Revealed

THE CHAMBER WAS VAST and circular, its walls lined with intricate carvings and runes that pulsed with a faint, sickly light. The floor was covered in a thick layer of dust, undisturbed by the passage of time. But it was the object in the center of the chamber that drew Elara's gaze—the Heart of the City.

The Heart was a massive crystal, easily as tall as Elara herself. It hovered a few feet above the ground, suspended in midair by some unseen force. The crystal's surface was smooth and flawless, its facets catching the faint light and refracting it into a thousand different shades of crimson. But it was the energy within the Heart that held Elara's attention—the dark, swirling magic that pulsed and throbbed like a living thing.

Elara could feel the power of the Heart radiating out from the crystal, filling the chamber with a sense of dread and unease. The air around the Heart seemed to shimmer and warp, as if reality itself was bending under the weight of its power.

But despite the fear that gnawed at her heart, Elara could not help but be captivated by the Heart's terrible beauty. It was a creation of immense power and complexity, a testament to the ingenuity and ambition of the city's people. But it was also a creation of darkness, a vessel for the malevolent forces that had brought about the city's destruction.

As Elara approached the Heart, she felt a strange sensation wash over her—a feeling of warmth and comfort, as if the crystal was reaching out to her, welcoming her presence. The sensation was so strong that it almost made her forget the danger that the Heart represented.

But as she reached out to touch the crystal, a voice filled her mind—a voice that was both soothing and terrifying in its intensity.

"Welcome, Elara," the voice said, its tone soft and seductive. "You have come far, and now you stand before the Heart of the City. You are strong, stronger than any who have come before you. But you could be so much more. The power of the Heart is yours to command. All you have to do is take it."

Elara froze, her hand hovering just inches away from the crystal's surface. The voice was like a siren's call, filling her mind with visions of grandeur and power. She saw herself standing at the head of a great army, her enemies falling before her as she wielded the power of the Heart. She saw herself ruling over a vast empire, her people worshipping her as a goddess. She saw herself unlocking the secrets of the universe, bending reality itself to her will.

The visions were so vivid, so tempting, that Elara felt herself drawn to the Heart, her hand slowly reaching out to touch the crystal's smooth surface. The power of the Heart was within her grasp, and all she had to do was take it.

But just as her fingers brushed against the crystal, Elara felt a jolt of pain, as if she had been struck by lightning. The visions shattered, replaced by a torrent of images and emotions—the fear and despair of the city's people as the curse consumed them, the regret and guilt of the leaders as they realized the extent of their mistake, the dark, malevolent presence of the curse as it fed on their suffering.

Elara pulled her hand away from the crystal, gasping for breath as the images and emotions faded from her mind. The Heart was not just a source of power—it was a source of corruption, a vessel for the dark forces that had brought about the city's destruction.

The voice in her mind grew more insistent, its tone filled with a mixture of anger and desperation. "Do not be a fool, Elara," the voice hissed. "The power of the Heart is beyond anything you can imagine. With it, you could reshape the world, bring about a new era of peace and prosperity. All you have to do is take it!"

Elara clenched her fists, her heart pounding with fear and determination. The Heart's power was immense, but it was also dangerous—too dangerous to be wielded by anyone. The curse that had been unleashed upon the city had been a result of the Heart's power, and she could not allow that power to be unleashed again.

With a deep breath, Elara summoned the blessings of the gods, feeling their warmth and strength flow through her. The fear and doubt that had been gnawing at her heart began to fade, replaced by a sense of resolve and determination.

"I will not be tempted by your lies," Elara said, her voice steady and firm. "The Heart of the City is a creation of darkness, and its power has only brought suffering and destruction. I will not allow it to corrupt me, or anyone else."

The voice in her mind screamed in rage, the power of the Heart surging as it tried to overwhelm her will. The crystal pulsed with a blinding light, its dark energies swirling faster and faster as the curse within it tried to break free.

But Elara held firm, her will unyielding as she channeled the blessings of the gods into the Heart. The warmth of the blessings filled her with a sense of peace and strength, pushing back against the darkness that threatened to consume her.

The battle between light and darkness raged within the chamber, the power of the Heart clashing with the blessings of the gods. The air was filled with a deafening roar as the energies collided, the very walls of the tower shaking with the force of their struggle.

But slowly, the power of the Heart began to wane, its dark energies faltering in the face of Elara's determination. The crystal's light grew dimmer, its pulsations growing weaker as the curse that had been unleashed upon the city was pushed back, its hold on the Heart weakening.

With a final, powerful surge of energy, Elara broke the Heart's hold, the crystal's light shattering as its dark energies were neutralized. The curse that had plagued the city for centuries was broken, its malevolent presence dissolving into nothingness as the Heart's power was finally extinguished.

The Aftermath

THE SILENCE THAT FOLLOWED was profound, the air filled with a sense of peace and tranquility that had not been felt in the city for centuries. The darkness that had permeated the tower was gone, replaced by a soft, golden light that seemed to emanate from the very walls.

Elara stood in the center of the chamber, her body trembling with exhaustion but her heart filled with a sense of triumph. The Heart of the City was gone, its dark magic neutralized and its curse lifted. The city that had been destroyed by its own hubris could finally find peace.

As she made her way out of the tower, Elara felt a sense of closure and fulfillment. The journey had been long and difficult, but she had achieved what she had set out to do. The curse had been broken, and the city's people could finally rest.

The streets of the forgotten city were bathed in a soft, golden light, the oppressive silence that had hung over the city replaced by the gentle rustling of leaves and the distant call of birds. The city was still a place of ruin and decay, but there was a sense of renewal in the air, as if the city was finally at peace.

Elara walked slowly through the streets, her eyes taking in the beauty of the city's architecture, the intricate carvings and delicate filigree that adorned its buildings. The city had been a place of greatness and tragedy, a reminder of the dangers of unchecked ambition and the importance of wisdom, compassion, and humility.

As she reached the city's gates, Elara turned to take one last look at the forgotten metropolis. The city had given her the answers she sought, and now it was time for her to take those lessons and use them to shape the future.

With a deep breath, Elara stepped out of the city and into the light of the outside world. The journey was far from over, but she knew that she was ready to face whatever challenges lay ahead.

The Heart of the City had been destroyed, its curse lifted, and the future was hers to shape.

Chapter 13: The Awakening

The Dawn of a New Era

Elara stepped out of the central tower and into the light of the early morning. The air was fresh and crisp, carrying with it the scent of dew-covered grass and blooming flowers. The heavy sense of dread that had once permeated the city was gone, replaced by a feeling of renewal and hope. The curse that had plagued the city for centuries had been broken, and now, as the first rays of sunlight touched the ancient stone structures, the city was beginning to awaken.

For a moment, Elara stood still, allowing herself to take in the transformation that was unfolding before her. The once oppressive silence had been replaced by the gentle sounds of nature. Birds sang from the tops of the ruined towers, their melodic voices echoing through the streets. The wind whispered through the leaves of the ivy and vines that had long since claimed the city's walls, carrying with it the promise of a new beginning.

The city, once a place of despair and desolation, now felt alive with a different kind of energy—an energy that was both ancient and new, filled with the promise of rebirth and renewal. Elara could feel it in the air, a pulsating rhythm that seemed to resonate with the very stones of the city, as if the ruins themselves were stirring from a long slumber.

The journey had been long and fraught with challenges, but now, standing in the light of a new dawn, Elara knew that it had all been worth it. The city was awakening, and she was about to witness the rebirth of a civilization that had once been lost to time.

The Spirits of the Lost Civilization

AS ELARA WALKED THROUGH the streets, she began to notice subtle changes in the city around her. The air seemed to shimmer with a soft, golden light, and the shadows that had once clung to the walls were now retreating, replaced by a warm, inviting glow. The ruins, once crumbling and overgrown, were beginning to repair themselves, the stones shifting and settling into place as if guided by an unseen hand.

But it was not just the physical city that was changing. As Elara continued to explore, she began to see the faint, ethereal forms of the spirits of the lost civilization. They appeared as shimmering silhouettes, their bodies composed of light and energy, their movements graceful and fluid. These were the souls of the people who had once lived in the city, the men and women who had built it, loved it, and ultimately been consumed by the curse that had destroyed it.

Elara watched in awe as the spirits moved through the streets, their presence bringing life back to the city. Some were engaged in what appeared to be daily tasks—sweeping the streets, tending to gardens, or repairing structures—while others simply walked, their faces filled with a sense of peace and fulfillment. It was as if the curse that had trapped them for so long had finally been lifted, allowing them to resume their lives, even in this ghostly form.

One spirit, a woman dressed in the flowing robes of a scholar, approached Elara. Her face was serene, her eyes filled with gratitude as she bowed slightly in greeting.

"Thank you," the spirit said, her voice soft and melodic, like the rustling of leaves in a gentle breeze. "You have freed us from the curse that bound us to this place. For centuries, we have wandered these streets, trapped in a cycle of despair and regret. But now, thanks to you, we are free."

Elara felt a lump form in her throat as she listened to the spirit's words. The weight of the journey, the trials she had faced, and the sacrifices she had made all came rushing back to her, but now they felt lighter, as if a great burden had been lifted from her shoulders.

"I did what I had to do," Elara replied, her voice trembling with emotion. "The city deserved a second chance, and so did its people."

The spirit nodded, her smile warm and kind. "And now, because of you, we have that chance. The city will rebuild itself, and we will once again be able to share the knowledge and wisdom that was lost so long ago."

Elara watched as the spirit turned and joined a group of others, who were gathering around one of the city's grand fountains. The fountain, once dry and overgrown with moss, was now flowing with crystal-clear water, its surface sparkling in the sunlight. The spirits dipped their hands into the water, their forms becoming more solid and defined with each passing moment.

It was as if the city itself was feeding off their energy, using it to repair the damage that had been done by the curse. The stones of the buildings began to mend themselves, the cracks sealing and the surfaces smoothing out as the structures slowly regained their former glory. The vines and ivy that had once choked the life out of the city were now retreating, their roots pulling back from the walls and returning to the earth.

Elara felt a sense of wonder and awe as she watched the city come back to life. The rebirth of the civilization was not just a physical reconstruction—it was a spiritual awakening, a restoration of the city's soul. The spirits of the lost civilization were no longer bound by the curse; they were free to rebuild their city, to share their knowledge and wisdom with future generations.

The Rebirth of the City

AS ELARA CONTINUED her journey through the city, she witnessed the full extent of its rebirth. The grand structures that had once been reduced to ruins were now standing tall and proud once more, their facades gleaming in the sunlight. The intricate carvings and delicate filigree that adorned the buildings had been restored to their original beauty, their details sharp and clear.

The streets, once choked with debris and overgrown with weeds, were now clear and clean, the cobblestones gleaming as if freshly laid. The fountains, which had long since dried up, were now flowing with water, their surfaces reflecting the light in a dazzling display of color.

The people of the city—the spirits who had been trapped by the curse—were now fully restored, their forms solid and lifelike. They moved through the streets with purpose, their faces filled with joy and contentment as they went about their daily lives. The city was alive with activity, a vibrant, bustling metropolis that was once again a beacon of hope and progress.

Elara felt a sense of pride and fulfillment as she watched the city come back to life. This was the culmination of her journey, the moment she had been working toward since she first set foot in the forgotten city. The knowledge and wisdom of the lost civilization had been restored, and the city was once again a place of beauty and wonder.

But even as the city rebuilt itself, Elara knew that there was still work to be done. The rebirth of the city was not just about restoring its physical structures—it was about ensuring that the mistakes of the past were not repeated. The curse that had destroyed the city had been born out of hubris and ambition, and it was up to her to ensure that the new civilization that arose from the ashes did not fall into the same trap.

As she made her way to the city's central square, Elara saw a group of the city's leaders gathered around a large, ornate table. These were the same leaders she had seen in the visions, the men and women who had guided the city through its greatest triumphs and its darkest days. But now, their faces were filled with a sense of peace and understanding, as if they had finally come to terms with the mistakes they had made.

One of the leaders, a man with a tall, commanding presence and a deep, resonant voice, stepped forward to address Elara.

"You have done what we could not," he said, his voice filled with gratitude. "You have freed us from the curse that we brought upon ourselves, and you have given us a second chance. We will not squander it. We will use the knowledge and wisdom that we have gained to build a better future, one that is guided by humility, compassion, and respect for the natural world."

Elara nodded, her heart filled with a sense of fulfillment. The leaders of the city had learned from their mistakes, and they were determined to build a civilization that would not repeat the errors of the past.

But even as the city's leaders spoke of the future, Elara knew that there was one final task that remained. The gods who had guided her through her journey had one last blessing to bestow upon the city and its new guardian.

The Blessing of the Gods

AS ELARA STOOD IN THE center of the square, the air around her began to shimmer with a soft, golden light. The light grew brighter and more intense, until it filled the entire square with a warm, radiant glow. The spirits of the city, the people who had once lived there, and the leaders who had guided it, all paused in their activities and turned their gaze toward the light, their faces filled with awe and reverence.

From the heart of the light, the forms of the gods began to materialize. They were magnificent beings, their bodies composed of light and energy, their forms both awe-inspiring and comforting. Each god represented a different aspect of the world—wisdom, strength, compassion, and more—and their presence filled the square with a sense of peace and tranquility.

Elara felt a sense of calm wash over her as the gods approached, their forms radiating a warmth that soothed her soul. These were the gods who had guided her through her journey, who had bestowed upon her the blessings that had given her the strength and resolve to break the curse.

The gods gathered around Elara, their eyes filled with pride and admiration. The god of wisdom, a figure with a serene, thoughtful expression and a robe of shimmering gold, stepped forward to address her.

"Elara," the god said, their voice soft and melodic, like the sound of a gentle breeze. "You have proven yourself to be a true guardian of this city. You have shown wisdom, strength, and compassion in the face of great challenges, and you have succeeded where others have failed."

The god of strength, a towering figure with muscles like steel and eyes that glowed with a fierce, protective light, stepped forward next. "You have faced the darkness and emerged victorious," the god said, their voice deep and resonant. "You have broken the curse that has plagued this city for centuries, and in doing so, you have restored hope and light to its people."

The god of compassion, a gentle, nurturing figure with a warm, comforting smile, also approached. "You have shown kindness and empathy to those in need," the god said, their voice filled with love and understanding. "You have helped to heal the wounds of the past, and you have brought peace to the spirits of this city."

Elara felt a lump form in her throat as she listened to the gods' words. The journey had been long and difficult, but hearing their praise made her realize just how far she had come. She had faced her deepest fears, confronted the darkness within herself, and emerged stronger and more determined.

The gods gathered around Elara, their forms glowing with a soft, golden light. "We have one final blessing to bestow upon you," the god of wisdom said. "You have proven yourself to be a true guardian of this city, and now we will grant you the power and knowledge to guide it into the future."

The gods raised their hands, and a beam of golden light shot down from the heavens, enveloping Elara in its warm embrace. The light filled her with a sense of peace and fulfillment, as if all the pieces of her journey had finally come together.

Elara closed her eyes as the light washed over her, feeling the power of the gods flowing through her. She felt stronger, more connected to the city and its people than ever before. The knowledge and wisdom of the lost civilization filled her mind, and she knew that she was ready to guide the city into a new era.

When the light finally faded, Elara opened her eyes to find herself standing in the center of the square, the gods surrounding her with smiles of approval. The spirits of the city had gathered around, their faces filled with awe and reverence as they watched the gods bestow their blessing upon her.

"You are now the guardian of this city," the god of wisdom said, their voice filled with pride. "You have the power and knowledge to guide it into the future, to ensure that the mistakes of the past are not repeated. Use this gift wisely, and may the city thrive under your guidance."

The gods began to fade, their forms dissolving into the golden light that had enveloped the square. But before they disappeared completely, the god of strength stepped forward one last time.

"Remember, Elara," the god said, their voice filled with a deep, resonant power. "The true strength of a leader lies not in their ability to wield power, but in their ability to inspire and uplift those around them. Lead with wisdom, compassion, and humility, and the city will prosper."

With those final words, the gods disappeared, leaving Elara standing alone in the square, the golden light slowly fading into the morning sun.

The New Guardian

AS THE LIGHT FADED, Elara felt a deep sense of peace and fulfillment. The gods had bestowed their blessing upon her, granting her the power and knowledge to guide the city into the future. The journey that had begun so long ago had finally come full circle, and she was ready to embrace her new role as the city's guardian.

The spirits of the city, now fully restored, gathered around Elara, their faces filled with admiration and gratitude. The leaders of the city, the men and women who had once guided it through its greatest triumphs and its darkest days, stepped forward to offer their support.

"You have been chosen by the gods," the leader with the commanding presence said, his voice filled with respect. "We are honored to follow your guidance and to help you rebuild this city into the beacon of hope and progress it was always meant to be."

Elara nodded, her heart filled with a sense of responsibility and purpose. She knew that the road ahead would not be easy, that there would be challenges and obstacles to overcome. But she also knew that she was not alone. The people of the city, the spirits who had been freed from the curse, were with her, and together, they would build a new civilization, one that was guided by the principles of wisdom, compassion, and humility.

As Elara stood in the center of the square, the city around her continued to rebuild itself, the structures rising from the ruins like phoenixes from the ashes. The knowledge and wisdom of the lost civilization had been restored, and the city was once again a place of beauty and wonder, a place where the past and the future converged.

The journey that had brought Elara to this point had been long and difficult, but it had also been a journey of growth and discovery. She had faced her deepest fears, confronted the darkness within herself, and emerged stronger and more determined. The gods had guided her every step of the way, and now they had entrusted her with the future of the city.

As the first rays of sunlight touched the city's spires, Elara felt a sense of hope and possibility. The city was awakening, and with it, a new era was dawning. The future was bright, and under her guidance, the city would thrive.

Elara looked out over the city, her heart filled with a sense of fulfillment and purpose. The journey was far from over, but she knew that she was ready to face whatever challenges lay ahead.

The city was hers to protect, and she would do so with all the strength, wisdom, and compassion she possessed. The curse had been broken, the city had been reborn, and a new era was about to begin.

And Elara, the new guardian of the city, would lead the way.

Chapter 14: The Return

The Journey Home

The path leading back to Elara's village was familiar, yet it felt different this time. As she walked the winding trails through the dense forests and across the rolling hills, the weight of her journey still lingered, but it was no longer burdensome. Instead, it was a source of strength, a reminder of the trials she had overcome and the wisdom she had gained.

The landscape, vibrant with the colors of late spring, seemed to welcome her return. The leaves of the trees whispered in the gentle breeze, and the flowers that dotted the meadows nodded as if in greeting. Even the birds in the sky seemed to sing a special tune, their melodies lifting Elara's spirits as she made her way home.

It had been many weeks since she had left her village, guided by the prophecy of the hidden realm and driven by a destiny she had barely understood at the time. The village had always been her home, a place of comfort and routine, but after everything she had experienced, she knew that she would return a different person. She was no longer the curious, untested young woman who had left in search of answers. She was now a hero, the one who had lifted the curse of the lost civilization, restored a forgotten city, and become its guardian.

The thought filled Elara with a sense of pride, but also humility. She had not sought out this role, but it had found her nonetheless. And now, as she approached the outskirts of her village, she felt a deep sense of responsibility. The knowledge and wisdom she carried with her were not just for her own benefit—they were gifts to be shared with her people, tools to forge a new era of prosperity and enlightenment.

The journey home was long, but it allowed Elara time to reflect on everything that had happened. She thought of the city's rebirth, the spirits she had freed, and the gods who had blessed her. Each memory was a testament to the strength and resilience she had discovered within herself, and to the power of knowledge and wisdom when guided by compassion and humility.

As the village came into view, nestled in the valley below, Elara felt a swell of emotion. This was her home, the place where she had been born and raised, the place where her journey had begun. And now, she was returning not just as a daughter of the village, but as its hero.

The Arrival

THE VILLAGERS WERE going about their daily routines when Elara first set foot back on the familiar paths of her homeland. The sun was high in the sky, casting a warm, golden light over the thatched-roof cottages and the fields of grain that surrounded the village. Children played near the edge of the forest, their laughter carrying on the breeze, while the adults tended to their work, unaware of the significant return that was about to take place.

As Elara walked through the fields and into the village, she was struck by the sense of normalcy that pervaded the place. Life had continued in her absence, just as it always had. The sight of familiar faces brought a smile to her lips, and yet there was also a twinge of sadness. So much had changed within her, but here, everything seemed just as it had been when she left.

It wasn't long before the first villager noticed her presence. An older woman, bent over a basket of freshly picked herbs, looked up and let out a gasp. Her eyes widened with recognition, and she dropped the basket, its contents spilling onto the ground as she rushed toward Elara.

"Elara! You've returned!" the woman cried, her voice filled with a mixture of disbelief and joy. "We feared you might never come back! What happened? Tell us, what did you find?"

Elara smiled, feeling the warmth of the woman's words. "I have much to tell," she replied gently. "But first, let us gather everyone. The story I bring is one that must be shared with all."

The woman nodded quickly and hurried off, calling out to the other villagers as she went. It wasn't long before a crowd began to gather in the village square, drawn by the news of Elara's return. The children abandoned their games, the farmers left their fields, and even the village elders emerged from their homes, their curiosity piqued.

As Elara stood in the center of the square, she looked around at the faces of the people she had known all her life. There were the friends she had played with as a child, the neighbors who had watched her grow up, and the elders who had taught her the traditions and stories of their people. These were the people she had fought for, the people who would benefit from the knowledge she had gained.

The crowd grew quiet as the village chief, a tall man with a mane of graying hair and wise, knowing eyes, stepped forward. He looked at Elara with a mixture of pride and relief, his weathered face softening into a smile.

"Welcome home, Elara," the chief said, his voice deep and resonant. "We have awaited your return with great anticipation. We knew that the journey you undertook was one of great importance, and now that you have returned, we are eager to hear what you have learned."

Elara nodded, feeling the weight of the moment settle upon her. She took a deep breath and began to speak.

The Tale of the Forgotten City

THE VILLAGERS LISTENED in rapt attention as Elara recounted her journey, beginning with the ancient prophecy that had been told among the elders of the village. She spoke of the hidden realm, the forgotten city buried deep within the mountains, and the trials she had faced along the way. Her words painted vivid images in the minds of her listeners, and they could almost see the towering spires of the city, the labyrinth of shadows, and the chamber of memories.

She told them of the curse that had been placed upon the city, a curse born of the people's own hubris and ambition. She described the Heart of the City, the powerful artifact that had granted the civilization immense power but had ultimately led to its destruction. The villagers gasped in horror as she recounted how the dark magic of the Heart had consumed the city, trapping its inhabitants in an eternal cycle of despair.

But Elara's tale did not end in tragedy. She spoke of her confrontation with the Heart, of how she had resisted its temptations and used the blessings of the gods to break the curse. She described the city's rebirth, how the spirits of the lost civilization had been freed and how the ruins had begun to rebuild themselves. The villagers listened with bated breath, their eyes wide with wonder as they imagined the forgotten city coming back to life before their very eyes.

As Elara spoke, she saw the faces of her people change. Where there had been fear and uncertainty, there was now hope and inspiration. The knowledge and wisdom she had brought back with her were not just stories—they were tools that could be used to shape the future of the village, to bring about a new era of prosperity and enlightenment.

When she finally finished her tale, the villagers erupted into applause and cheers. The children laughed and clapped their hands, while the adults exchanged looks of amazement and admiration. The village chief stepped forward once more, his eyes shining with pride.

"Elara, you have done more than we could have ever imagined," he said, his voice filled with emotion. "You have not only lifted the curse of the forgotten city, but you have also brought back knowledge and wisdom that will benefit our people for generations to come. You are a hero, not just to us, but to all who will hear your story."

Elara felt her cheeks flush with warmth as the villagers crowded around her, offering their congratulations and gratitude. But even as she basked in their praise, she knew that her work was not yet done. The knowledge she had gained from the forgotten city was vast, and it would take time to share it with her people and to help them understand how to use it to improve their lives.

But for now, she allowed herself to enjoy the moment, to revel in the joy of being home and the satisfaction of knowing that she had made a difference.

A New Era of Prosperity

IN THE DAYS AND WEEKS that followed, Elara worked tirelessly to share the knowledge and wisdom she had brought back from the forgotten city. She met with the village elders, discussing the ancient technologies and practices that had been lost to time, and together they devised ways to adapt them to the needs of their people.

One of the first changes Elara introduced was a new method of agriculture, based on the techniques she had learned from the city's spirits. The village's fields, once subject to the whims of the weather and the limitations of traditional farming practices, began to flourish as the new methods took root. Crops grew faster and more abundantly, and the village's granaries soon overflowed with food.

The villagers marveled at the transformation, and word of Elara's success spread to neighboring communities. People from other villages began to visit, seeking to learn the secrets of the newfound prosperity. Elara welcomed them with open arms, sharing her knowledge freely and encouraging them to adopt the practices that had brought such bounty to her own village.

But it wasn't just the fields that benefited from Elara's wisdom. She also introduced new methods of building and craftsmanship, drawing on the intricate designs and techniques she had seen in the forgotten city. The villagers began to construct stronger, more durable homes, using materials and methods that had been lost to time. The thatched-roof cottages were replaced with sturdy stone dwellings, their walls adorned with carvings that told the story of the village's history and its connection to the forgotten city.

The village itself underwent a transformation, evolving from a small, isolated community into a thriving center of learning and trade. The knowledge and wisdom that Elara had brought back attracted scholars, artisans, and traders from far and wide, all eager to contribute to the village's growth and prosperity.

The village chief, recognizing the importance of what was happening, declared that the village would become a place of learning, where people from all walks of life could come to study and share their knowledge. A grand library was built in the center of the village, filled with books and scrolls that chronicled the wisdom of the forgotten civilization, as well as the new discoveries and innovations that were being made by the villagers.

Elara spent much of her time in the library, guiding the scholars and scribes who came to study the ancient texts. She knew that the knowledge she had brought back was vast, and it would take many lifetimes to fully understand

and apply it. But she also knew that she had laid the foundation for something greater, something that would benefit her people for generations to come.

The village, once a small and humble community, had become a beacon of enlightenment and prosperity. The people who lived there were no longer just farmers and craftsmen—they were scholars, inventors, and leaders, all working together to build a better future.

And at the heart of it all was Elara, the hero who had returned from the forgotten city with the knowledge and wisdom that had transformed their lives.

A Celebration of Return

THE VILLAGERS WERE not content to let Elara's achievements go unrecognized. They decided to hold a grand celebration in her honor, a festival that would not only mark her return but also celebrate the new era of prosperity that she had brought to the village.

The preparations for the festival began weeks in advance. The villagers decorated the streets with colorful banners and flowers, and the aroma of freshly baked bread and roasted meats filled the air. Musicians tuned their instruments, and dancers practiced their steps, all eager to showcase their talents at the celebration.

On the day of the festival, the village square was filled with people, not just from Elara's village but from neighboring communities as well. Word of Elara's return had spread far and wide, and people from all over the region had come to celebrate the hero who had restored the legends of the lost civilization.

The village chief, dressed in his finest robes, stood at the entrance to the square, welcoming the guests as they arrived. He had prepared a special speech for the occasion, one that would honor Elara and recognize the impact she had made on the village and its people.

As the sun began to set, casting a warm, golden light over the village, the chief called for silence. The crowd grew quiet, their eyes turning toward the stage that had been set up in the center of the square. Elara stood at the front of the stage, her heart pounding with a mixture of excitement and nervousness as she prepared to address the crowd.

The chief stepped forward, raising his hands to the sky as he began his speech. "My friends," he said, his voice carrying across the square. "Today, we come together to celebrate a remarkable woman, a hero who has brought light and knowledge to our village. Elara's journey to the forgotten city is a tale that will be told for generations to come, a story of courage, wisdom, and the triumph of the human spirit."

The crowd erupted into applause, their cheers echoing through the village. Elara smiled, feeling a deep sense of gratitude for the support and love of her people.

"But Elara's journey was not just about lifting a curse," the chief continued. "It was about bringing back the knowledge and wisdom of a lost civilization, about restoring the legacy of our ancestors and ensuring that their lessons are not forgotten. Because of her, we now stand on the threshold of a new era, one that is filled with promise and possibility."

The chief turned to Elara, his eyes filled with pride. "Elara, you have given us more than we could have ever imagined. You have shown us that the past is not something to be feared, but something to be learned from, something that can guide us as we build a better future. On behalf of the village, I want to thank you for everything you have done. You are not just a hero—you are our leader, our guide, and our inspiration."

The crowd erupted into applause once more, and Elara felt tears welling up in her eyes as she listened to the chief's words. She had always known that her journey would be important, but she had never imagined that it would have such a profound impact on her people.

As the applause died down, the chief gestured for Elara to step forward. "Now," he said, "I invite Elara to share a few words with us."

Elara took a deep breath and stepped to the front of the stage, her heart pounding with a mixture of nerves and excitement. She looked out at the crowd, at the faces of the people who had supported her throughout her journey, and felt a deep sense of connection to each and every one of them.

"Thank you," Elara began, her voice steady and clear. "Thank you for your love, your support, and your belief in me. When I left this village, I had no idea what I would find, or what challenges I would face. But I knew that I was not alone. I knew that I carried with me the hopes and dreams of all of you, and that gave me the strength to keep going, even when things seemed impossible."

Elara paused, taking a moment to collect her thoughts. "The journey I undertook was not just about lifting a curse—it was about discovering who we are as a people, about reconnecting with our past and using that knowledge to build a better future. The forgotten city was a place of wonder and beauty, but it was also a place of great tragedy. The people there made mistakes, mistakes that led to their downfall. But from those mistakes, we can learn valuable lessons, lessons that will guide us as we move forward."

Elara looked out at the crowd, her eyes filled with determination. "We have been given a great gift—a gift of knowledge and wisdom that will help us create a better future for ourselves and for future generations. But with that gift comes responsibility. It is up to us to use that knowledge wisely, to ensure that we do not repeat the mistakes of the past."

The crowd was silent, hanging on her every word. Elara could feel the weight of their expectations, but she also felt a deep sense of purpose. This was what she had been meant to do, what the gods had guided her toward from the very beginning.

"I am honored to stand before you today," Elara continued, her voice filled with emotion. "But this is not just my journey—it is our journey. Together, we will build a new future, one that is guided by wisdom, compassion, and humility. We will take the lessons of the past and use them to create a world that is better than the one we have known. And I am proud to be a part of that journey, alongside all of you."

The crowd erupted into applause once more, and Elara felt a deep sense of fulfillment as she stepped back from the stage. The celebration that followed was filled with joy and laughter, as the villagers came together to honor Elara and to celebrate the new era of prosperity and enlightenment that she had brought to their village.

The Legacy of Elara

AS THE FESTIVAL CONTINUED late into the night, Elara took a moment to step away from the crowd and reflect on everything that had happened. She stood on a hill overlooking the village, the lights of the celebration twinkling like stars in the distance. The moon hung low in the sky, casting a soft, silvery light over the landscape.

Elara thought about the journey she had undertaken, the challenges she had faced, and the lessons she had learned. She knew that the knowledge and wisdom she had brought back from the forgotten city would have a lasting impact on her people, but she also knew that her work was far from over.

The new era that had begun was just the beginning, and there would be much to do in the days, months, and years ahead. Elara was determined to continue her work, to ensure that the knowledge of the lost civilization was preserved and that her people continued to learn and grow.

But for now, as she stood on the hill, she allowed herself to feel a sense of peace and contentment. She had done what she had set out to do, and she had returned home with more than just stories—she had returned with the tools to build a better future.

As Elara looked out over the village, she knew that her legacy would be more than just the tale of her journey. It would be the knowledge she had brought back, the wisdom she had shared, and the lives she had touched.

And in that moment, Elara knew that she was exactly where she was meant to be.

The village was her home, and she was its guardian, its guide, and its inspiration. Together, they would build a new future, one that honored the past while embracing the possibilities of tomorrow.

And so, with the moonlight guiding her steps, Elara turned and walked back toward the village, ready to embrace whatever the future might hold.

Chapter 15: The Legacy of the Forgotten City

The Weight of Reflection

Elara sat at the edge of the village's central square, her gaze fixed on the horizon where the first hints of dawn were beginning to touch the sky. The village was quiet, the air still and peaceful in the early morning light. The celebration of her return and the village's newfound prosperity had finally quieted down, and now, in the silence, she found herself alone with her thoughts.

The journey she had undertaken to the forgotten city felt both distant and immediate, like a dream that had etched itself deeply into her soul. The memory of each trial, each encounter, and each revelation played in her mind like a sequence of still images, vibrant with the emotions they had evoked. The city's haunting beauty, the eerie silence of its ruins, the powerful presence of the Heart, and the rebirth she had witnessed—they were all woven together into a tapestry that formed the story of her journey.

Yet, as she sat there, reflecting on everything that had happened, Elara realized that the true journey had not been merely one of discovery or of breaking a curse. It had been a journey of understanding—of herself, of her people, and of the civilization that had risen to great heights only to fall into ruin. The city had been a place of wonder, filled with knowledge and technology far beyond what her village had ever known, but it had also been a place where ambition had outstripped wisdom, where power had been pursued without regard for the consequences.

The legacy of the forgotten city was not in its wealth or its power, but in the lessons it had left behind. The city's rise and fall had been a cautionary tale, a reminder of the dangers of hubris and the importance of humility, compassion, and balance. These were the treasures she had brought back with her, more valuable than any physical artifact or relic.

As the sky began to lighten, Elara knew that it was time to pass on what she had learned, to ensure that the legacy of the forgotten city would not be lost again. The knowledge she had gained was not hers to keep—it was a gift that needed to be shared, a foundation upon which the future could be built.

The Lessons of the Past

THE FIRST STEP IN PASSING on the legacy of the forgotten city was to ensure that its lessons were understood by the people of the village. Elara knew that the villagers looked up to her, that they saw her as a hero who had returned with the secrets of an ancient civilization. But she also knew that it was not enough for them to admire her—they needed to understand the full scope of what she had learned.

In the days that followed, Elara spent countless hours in the village's new library, working with the scholars and scribes who had come from near and far to study the knowledge she had brought back. Together, they compiled the stories, the teachings, and the technologies of the forgotten city, transcribing them into books and scrolls that would be preserved for future generations.

But Elara was careful to ensure that the focus was not just on the city's achievements. She emphasized the importance of understanding the reasons for the city's downfall, the dangers of unchecked ambition, and the need for balance in all things. The books that were created were not just records of a lost civilization—they were guides for building a better future.

As the village's library grew, so too did its reputation as a center of learning and wisdom. People from across the region came to study, to share their own knowledge, and to learn from the lessons of the past. The village, once a small and isolated community, became a hub of enlightenment, a place where the legacy of the forgotten city lived on in the minds and hearts of those who sought to understand it.

But Elara knew that knowledge alone was not enough. The true legacy of the forgotten city would be measured not in books and scrolls, but in the actions of the people who had learned its lessons. It was not enough to simply know the dangers of hubris—they had to live by the principles of humility, compassion, and balance in their everyday lives.

To that end, Elara worked closely with the village leaders, guiding them in applying the lessons of the forgotten city to the challenges they faced. Together, they established new practices and policies that promoted fairness, sustainability, and the well-being of all members of the community. The village became a model of what a society could be when it was guided by wisdom and compassion, rather than by the pursuit of power and wealth.

The Next Generation

AS THE YEARS PASSED, Elara watched as the village continued to grow and prosper. The children who had once played in the fields were now young adults, eager to take on the responsibilities of leadership and to contribute to the ongoing development of their community. Elara knew that these young people would be the ones to carry the legacy of the forgotten city into the future, and she made it her mission to ensure that they were prepared for the task.

Elara took on the role of a mentor, teaching the next generation about the history of the forgotten city, its achievements, and its failures. She encouraged them to think critically, to question assumptions, and to seek out the truth for themselves. She taught them the importance of balance—of knowing when to push forward and when to step back, of recognizing the limits of their own knowledge and the need to listen to others.

One of the young people who stood out to Elara was a girl named Liora. Liora had been just a child when Elara had left on her journey, but now she was a bright and curious young woman with a passion for learning and a deep respect for the wisdom of the past. Liora reminded Elara of herself at that age—eager to explore, to understand, and to make a difference in the world.

Liora often sought Elara's guidance, asking questions about the forgotten city and the lessons it had to offer. She was particularly interested in the balance between progress and sustainability, and she spent hours in the library, studying the ancient texts and discussing her ideas with Elara and the other scholars.

One day, as they sat together in the shade of an old oak tree, Liora turned to Elara with a thoughtful expression.

"Elara," she began, "I've been thinking a lot about the forgotten city and the choices its people made. They had so much knowledge and power, but they lost sight of what was truly important. How can we make sure that we don't make the same mistakes? How can we balance progress with the need to protect what we have?"

Elara smiled, proud of the young woman's insight. "That's the key question, Liora," she replied. "It's not an easy one to answer, but I believe the answer lies in understanding our limitations and recognizing that we are part of a larger whole. Progress is important, but it must be guided by wisdom and tempered by compassion. We must always ask ourselves: How will our actions affect others? How will they affect the world around us? If we can keep those questions in mind, we can avoid the pitfalls that led to the downfall of the forgotten city."

Liora nodded thoughtfully. "I understand," she said. "But it's not just about us, is it? We have to teach others to think this way too, to ensure that these lessons are passed down through the generations."

Elara's heart swelled with pride. "Exactly," she said. "The legacy of the forgotten city is not something that can be preserved in a book or a building. It's something that must be lived, something that must be carried forward by each generation. And that's why it's so important that we continue to learn, to grow, and to teach others."

Liora smiled, a look of determination in her eyes. "I promise, Elara," she said. "I will do everything I can to ensure that the lessons of the forgotten city are never forgotten. I will teach them to others, just as you have taught them to me."

Elara reached out and placed a hand on Liora's shoulder. "I know you will," she said warmly. "And I have no doubt that you will make a difference, just as the people of the forgotten city once did. But remember, Liora—your journey is your own. You will face challenges and make choices that will shape your path. Trust in your own wisdom, and never be afraid to seek out the truth."

Liora nodded, her resolve unwavering. "Thank you, Elara," she said. "I will do my best."

As Elara watched Liora walk away, she felt a deep sense of fulfillment. The next generation was ready, and she knew that they would carry the legacy of the forgotten city into the future with the same care and wisdom that she had strived to impart.

The Eternal Legacy

AS THE YEARS PASSED, Elara continued to play a central role in the village's development, but she also began to take a step back, allowing the next generation to take on more responsibility. She watched with pride as Liora and others like her rose to positions of leadership, guiding the village with the wisdom and compassion that had become its defining characteristics.

The village itself had grown into a thriving community, a place where knowledge and learning were valued above all else. The library had expanded into a grand institution, attracting scholars from across the region who came to study the ancient texts and to share their own knowledge. The village had become a beacon of enlightenment, a place where the legacy of the forgotten city was not only preserved but celebrated.

But even as the village prospered, Elara knew that the true legacy of the forgotten city was not in the physical structures or the books that lined the library's shelves. It was in the values that had been instilled in the people—the understanding that true progress comes not from the pursuit of power, but from the pursuit of wisdom, compassion, and balance.

ELARA SPENT HER FINAL years reflecting on her journey and the impact it had had on her people. She wrote her own account of the journey, not just as a record of what had happened, but as a guide for those who would come after her. She wanted to ensure that the lessons she had learned would not be lost, that the story of the forgotten city would continue to inspire future generations.

One of the final acts of her life was to establish a tradition that would ensure the legacy of the forgotten city would never be forgotten. Each year, on the anniversary of her return to the village, the people would gather in the square to hear the story of the forgotten city, to reflect on its lessons, and to renew their commitment to the values that had guided their community.

The tradition became known as the Day of Reflection, and it was a time of celebration, learning, and renewal. The villagers would share stories, hold discussions, and recommit themselves to the principles of wisdom, compassion, and balance. It was a day to remember the past, but also to look forward to the future, to ensure that the lessons of the forgotten city would continue to guide them in the years to come.

Passing the Torch

AS ELARA'S TIME ON earth drew to a close, she knew that she had fulfilled her purpose. She had lifted the curse of the forgotten city, restored its legacy, and ensured that its lessons would live on in the hearts and minds of her people. But she also knew that her journey was just one chapter in a much larger story, one that would continue long after she was gone.

On her final day, Elara gathered the village's leaders, scholars, and young people around her. She spoke to them one last time, her voice filled with the wisdom of a lifetime of learning and experience.

"My dear friends," she began, her voice steady and clear. "It has been the greatest honor of my life to serve as the guardian of this village and the keeper of the legacy of the forgotten city. But now, it is time for me to pass the torch to you. The future is in your hands, and I have every confidence that you will carry it forward with the same wisdom, compassion, and balance that has guided us all."

She turned to Liora, who had grown into a wise and capable leader. "Liora," she said, "you have been like a daughter to me, and I am so proud of the person you have become. I know that you will continue to guide this village with the same care and thoughtfulness that you have always shown. The legacy of the forgotten city is now yours to protect and to pass on to the next generation."

Liora nodded, tears in her eyes. "I will do my best, Elara," she said. "I promise."

Elara smiled, her heart filled with peace. "I know you will," she said. "And I know that the future is bright, because it is in the hands of people like you."

With those final words, Elara closed her eyes, her spirit filled with a deep sense of fulfillment and contentment. She had lived a life of purpose, a life that had made a difference in the world. And as she took her final breath, she knew that the legacy of the forgotten city would live on, carried forward by the people she had loved and guided.

The Legend Lives On

ELARA'S PASSING WAS marked by a time of mourning, but also by a time of reflection and celebration. The village came together to honor her life and the impact she had made on their community. They held a grand ceremony in the square, where they shared stories of her journey, her wisdom, and the lessons she had imparted.

But even as they mourned her loss, the villagers knew that Elara's spirit would live on in the legacy she had left behind. The Day of Reflection became an even more important tradition, a time to remember not just the forgotten city, but also the woman who had brought its lessons to light.

As the years passed, Elara's story became a legend, passed down from generation to generation. The village continued to thrive, guided by the principles of wisdom, compassion, and balance that she had taught them. The library grew into a great center of learning, attracting scholars from across the world who came to study the ancient texts and to learn from the wisdom of the past.

But more than that, the legacy of the forgotten city became a living part of the village's culture, a guiding light that shaped their decisions and their actions. The people of the village knew that true progress came not from the pursuit of power, but from the pursuit of wisdom, compassion, and balance. And they were determined to pass those values on to their children and their children's children, ensuring that the lessons of the past would never be forgotten.

The story of Elara and the forgotten city was more than just a tale of adventure and discovery—it was a story of transformation, of growth, and of the power of knowledge and wisdom to shape the future. It was a story that would continue to inspire and guide the people of the village for generations to come.

And so, as the sun set on the village, casting a golden light over the fields and the rooftops, the people gathered in the square to hear the story once more. They listened with rapt attention as the village's storyteller recounted the tale of Elara's journey, her confrontation with the Heart of the City, and the rebirth of the forgotten civilization.

As the story came to an end, the storyteller looked out at the crowd and smiled. "And so, the legacy of the forgotten city lives on," she said. "It lives in our hearts, in our minds, and in the choices we make every day. It is a legacy of wisdom, compassion, and balance—a legacy that will guide us as we build a better future."

The villagers nodded in agreement, their hearts filled with a sense of purpose and pride. They knew that they were the guardians of the legacy, that it was up to them to ensure that it was never forgotten.

And so, with the setting sun casting its warm light over the village, the people of Elara's village reaffirmed their commitment to the legacy of the forgotten city. They knew that the journey was far from over, but they were ready to face whatever challenges lay ahead, guided by the wisdom of the past and the hope for the future.

Elara's story had come to an end, but the legacy she had left behind would continue to shape the world for generations to come.

And in that legacy, the forgotten city would never be forgotten again.

Don't miss out!

Visit the website below and you can sign up to receive emails whenever Patrick William Lee publishes a new book. There's no charge and no obligation.

https://books2read.com/r/B-A-FLRYB-WGIYE

Did you love *The Forgotten City*? Then you should read *The Enchanted Mirror*[1] by Patrick William Lee!

In "The Enchanted Mirror: A Tale of Destiny," a humble villager named Elara is thrust into a journey to fulfill an ancient prophecy. Guided by a magical mirror that reveals one's true destiny, Elara and her companions face trials that test their courage, wisdom, and loyalty. As they confront dark forces and hidden truths, Elara must embrace her destiny and lead her kingdom to peace. The story culminates in a final confrontation, where the prophecy is fulfilled in an unexpected way, leaving readers with a sense of closure and hope for the future.

1. https://books2read.com/u/bpA0pk

2. https://books2read.com/u/bpA0pk

About the Author

Patrick William Lee is a renowned author celebrated for his enchanting tales of magic and wonder. Specializing in the genres of fairy tales, folk tales, legends, and mythology, Patrick weaves stories that transport readers to fantastical realms where the impossible becomes reality. With a deep love for folklore and a talent for crafting timeless narratives, his books captivate the imaginations of readers young and old. When he's not writing, Patrick enjoys exploring ancient forests, studying mythical creatures, and sharing his passion for storytelling with audiences around the world. His works continue to inspire and delight, leaving a lasting impact on the world of literature.